# ALL THE WAY TO
# **HOME**

By

Jeanne L. Drouillard

Copyright © 2006 by Jeanne L. Drouillard

ISBN  0-7414-3161-0

*Published by:*

**INFI∞ITY**
PUBLISHING.COM

*1094 New DeHaven Street, Suite 100*
*West Conshohocken, PA 19428-2713*
*Info@buybooksontheweb.com*
*www.buybooksontheweb.com*
*Toll-free  (877) BUY BOOK*
*Local Phone (610) 941-9999*
*Fax  (610) 941-9959*

*Printed in the United States of America*

*Printed on Recycled Paper*

*Published  April 2008*

Dedicated to:

All the wonderful and brave children

Who allowed me inside their world

To share their Fears, Limitations,

Hopes and Realities

# TABLE OF CONTENTS

# SECTION I

# THE STORY OF LINDSEY HALL

# Chapter One

Cindy Hall entered April Munson's special-needs classroom that eighth day of September with her six-year old adopted daughter Lindsey. Try as she may she could not keep her from twisting and turning in her spot on the floor, as her bright blue eyes quickly took in all of the activities of the room. Cindy waited, somewhat impatiently, for her turn in line. Keeping Lindsey in a pleasant frame of mind was difficult anytime but today it was even more challenging. She was nervously trying to inch her way closer to her daughter, mostly for appearance sake, but her stubborn youngster would have none of it and for every inch that she moved in closer to her, her child moved away. She tried to grab her hand at one point and Lindsey immediately locked her arms behind her back as she looked defiantly into her mother's eyes with an obvious pout on her face.

"I want to go to the other school, mom. I don't like it here," Lindsey said on the verge of tears.

"If you improve at this school, then next year you can probably go back to Truman's Elementary school," said Cindy trying to speak kindly to her daughter, although the frustration of the last year or so always crept into her voice.

"But I want to go back there now. Why do I have to come to this place?"

Cindy knew that her little one didn't understand what was wrong and, to be honest, Cindy felt she didn't know either. "I can't take you back there this year, remember? They said you had to go to a special school first. And then, maybe, you could return for Grade 2."

"They're not nice over there. They don't like me. Why don't they like me?"

Cindy saw a very confused child looking up at her for answers. And she didn't have any. When Lindsey wasn't in one of her many unpredictable rages, she still needed to be watched. But there were occasional times that she could almost seem like a typical child. Unfortunately, she wasn't a typical child and she was growing more and more volatile.

"I don't want to be here. I don't want to be here. I don't want to be here," continued Lindsey.

Evaluating the incident with one glance, April realized immediately the frustration that both Lindsey and her mother were experiencing.

As she approached them and introduced herself, Lindsey announced immediately, "I don't want to be here. My mom says I have to come but you can't tell me what to do."

"Okay, Lindsey, maybe you and I can just discuss things," April said as she watched Lindsey give her a blatant stare, putting her hands on her hips and pursing her mouth tightly while she stood defiantly waiting for a response. She had spoken to April in such a rude and angry tone that it was half-expected she would begin stomping her little feet on the floor as a definite conclusion to her rather demanding performance. "Why don't you choose yourself a seat, Lindsey?" April said, never losing eye contact and watching her reaction to being given a choice, while responding minimally to her challenging behavior. Lindsey turned away, immediately claiming her independence.

Cindy said, "I tried to prepare her for coming to a different school, but she's been upset about it. I hope she settles down a little. "

"And if she doesn't, I'll see her using her disturbing behavior, which is what I need to see anyway. I know you're worried, Mrs. Hall, but we aren't going to reject her for bad behavior like a regular school. All the children here have behavior problems." April smiled at Cindy as best she could to reassure her, but she saw a very worried and frantic mother.

As Cindy looked over at Lindsey, April heard her say, "I sure hope that you can do something. Today was a very tough morning for her, so far. She didn't want to come, as you can tell. Anything outside her usual routine sets her off."

"Don't worry Mrs. Hall. That's what this class is about. Give us some time to work with her. And you know she'll be safe with us. My assistant Joanne Buckley and myself are both quite experienced with these type of children."

"Thanks Ms. Munson," said Cindy, and as she slowly turned to leave, she called out over her shoulder, "Good Luck."

Lindsey chose the last seat in the back of the classroom, although all of the other children were sitting up in the front. Looking around the room, she saw that it was pretty and painted in bright colors, with regular desks just like her other school and it had three big windows that let you see outside easily.

"Why don't you sit up here?" said the voice of one child.

"No," was all Lindsey cared to say.

"Oh, come on," came another voice.

"Leave me alone," she replied rather roughly and quite unpleasantly. After that no other children tried to tempt her forward.

At one point, a few kids turned around staring at her sitting all by herself at the back. Lindsey stuck her tongue out at them thinking they were probably making fun of her. *Why do I have to be here? I don't know these kids and I don't like them. They'll never be my friends. Stupid kids asking me to join them in front. I'd rather be by myself. They make me mad.*

Staring at April from the back of the room, Lindsey thought that she looked a little older than her mom but she was pretty. Her reddish blonde hair was short and her deep blue eyes made it seem that she could look right through you, like earlier when she's been talking to her. It made her want to run and hide. She thought her teacher seemed friendly though and she smiled a lot. Lindsey wouldn't admit it to another living soul, but she liked the fact that her teacher smiled a lot.

All of a sudden everyone turned around staring at her, including her teacher, as Lindsey had begun pounding her feet loudly on the floor. She had acquired this habit not only when she wanted attention but also when she was confused or anxious.

"Do you want something, Lindsey?" the teacher said rather loudly, since she was in the back of the room.

"What am I supposed to do? Tell me." Lindsey felt so alone but her pride would not let her accept any invitation to move forward.

"Attention everybody. First of all," said April as she addressed the entire class, "I want all of you to call me Ms.

April and my assistant here is Ms. Joanne. Right now we're going to introduce ourselves to each other. It can be your turn if you like, Lindsey. What would you like to tell the other children about yourself?"

"Nothing," answered Lindsey, looking down at the floor.

"I'm sure you mean 'Nothing, Ms. April.' Please try again, Lindsey."

"Nothing, ah, Ms. April." Lindsey added the title begrudgingly, "Don't want them to know nothing 'bout me."

"What about how old you are? Would you tell us how old you are, Lindsey?"

"No," said Lindsey haughtily.

"Probably don't know," replied Johnny, "girls aren't smart like boys." Lindsey knew immediately that Johnny didn't like girls and probably enjoyed hurting them. She couldn't let him win.

"You're stupid and you're small, and who'd listen to you anyway," she answered because truly she didn't much like girls or boys.

The bantering was allowed for a few moments and then her teacher stepped in with, "Everyone quiet please. Now actually children, you've just learned a lot about each other. We know Johnny thinks boys are smarter than girls and we know that Lindsey doesn't think Johnny is very smart. Would you like to add something, Anita?"

"Well, I think I'm smart but I don't count very well. But I try." Anita seemed shy and timid in her speech.

"You're a girl and you won't ever count good," replied

6

Johnny laughing. Lindsey knew his type and he would never miss an opportunity to put down girls, but she surprisingly saw Anita making an ugly face at him and thought, *Good for her.*

"Some um things are um just harder for um some people," said Matthew wanting to become part of the discussion.

"I know I (pause) want to learn (pause) and I will," said Jimmy, adding his own comment.

"I'm seven and just had a birthday last week," said Peter, shyly.

"Thank you, children. I'm sure that all of you will learn a lot about yourselves and each other this year and now we're all going to form a group and walk around the room together and I'll explain things to you. You can ask all the questions you want."

As the tour began April pointed out the different shaped bookshelves that lined three of the four walls, all in different colors, with so many different books that Anita commented, "Are we in a library?" "We don't have to read all of these books, do we?" added Johnny. "That's a lot of books," commented one of the others. "No, you don't have to read all of the books, but during free time, you're certainly welcome to look at any of the books you like. They have a lot of nice pictures and stories and we'll use some of them in our class work."

The room was happy-looking for a classroom and it had a lot of other things too like toys, paints, and different pictures. One entire wall was an aquarium with many unusual fish, most of which the children had never seen. April was happy to hear a question from Lindsey asking about some of the strange looking ones and where they had come from. Another wall had a huge blackboard with chalk in pastel colors. Most of the children enjoyed the tour as their curiosity kept their behavior in check. All made some comment or asked a question. They were trying to get used to their new classmates and their new surroundings but soon the newness would wear off and April had to be ready.

Making it through the first day, April wanted to review the files of her six special students. All had been refused attendance in regular school because of difficulty showing proper behavior on a regular basis. Some needed tender nudges to return their personality to normal developmental stages and some were more dangerous to themselves than others, and causes needed to be found along with remedies, or regular school would not be possible for them. Meeting the children today had made an impression on April, and now she needed to read their files again to remind herself of their individual needs.

Calling over her assistant, April felt very fortunate to have her return for her second year of student teaching. They had worked well in the past, thought alike and both had a passion for the special-needs children.

"We sure have a feisty group this year, don't we?" said Joanne.

"There will definitely be some challenges; I can guarantee that. But if we can find out about their internal conflicts, that's the key. They all have a good chance of making it next year since no one has permanent brain problems. And no one has FAS (Fetal Alcohol Syndrome) this year and I'm glad about that. Mental lag because of emotional trouble is entirely different. It's still never a quick fix but we have a much better chance." She read from Anita Bradley's file.

<u>Anita Bradley:</u> suffered physical and sexual abuse from

her father for almost a year before her mother found out. Charges were pressed by the mother but much harm had been done. Anita urinates in her bed at night, on purpose, to relieve her anger and rage, which she usually keeps inside causing her tremendous damage. She has made great strides with a loving mother, therapy, but she still unconsciously can't control her bladder at times indicating more unresolved anger. Prognosis: blurry, wait and see after special needs class.

"This bedwetting" began April, "is very different than an ordinary child who has the problem for a time, usually because they sleep too soundly and don't wake up. Anita wakes up and then pees in her bed on purpose because she's so angry. And the strange part is that this is not necessarily a conscious decision. She doesn't know that she can stop it, at least not yet. When young children are abused as she was, I find a situation where you have to watch for clues. No one knows how that child feels inside and she's too young to explain it. She's letting the world know something is very wrong. You want to just go up to her and hug all the pain out of her but that's not the answer. That innocent face can't deter us from helping her and nudging her along in the right direction."

"She seems so delicate and outwardly you'd never guess her anger and pain. How do you fix a child like that?" asked Joanne.

"She has a good strong mother, a loving grandmother and her therapist is long on patience. I know her. She'll make it but it will take time. The type of abuse she endured stays inside for a long time and usually never goes away completely. But she'll learn to live with it. Sad, isn't it? But that's the best we can do. Others have learned to live with it but they never forget. How could they?"

"Matthew and Jimmy are progressing nicely, don't you

think April? What a shock they must have had."

<u>Matthew Culvert</u>):
<u>Jimmy McKnight</u>): both quite normal first graders until they witnessed their neighbor shot to death by a drive-by shooter in the front yard next door to them. Neither one talked for almost a month and then Matthew's speech was very slurry in his first attempts while Jimmy could only talk with long pauses between his words. Their concentration is still quite difficult and they can be slow to answer questions or follow instructions. But they've made good progress in the last six months. <u>Prognosis:</u> One year of special class should allow them to return to regular school.

"Yeah and it's good that we can keep them together for a while," added April. "They're so many things that can be resolved best by feeling connections and not in words and they're actually helping each other to heal as much as any therapist. The human being is such an amazing creation."

"I hear some philosophy coming up again," Joanne laughed.

"Well, I'm glad I've got you back this year. I think we understand each other. How much longer before you graduate?"

"Two more years. I want to get the same qualifications that you have. I've signed up for the extra teaching certificate. Some day I may have a classroom down the hall from you."

"Wouldn't that be great? You're wonderful Joanne. Truly a pleasure to work with."

"But you're my hero. I was going to be a math teacher for seventh or eighth grade, remember? And then they gave me your class for training with these special children. It was a lucky day for me and it changed my life. This is what I want to do too."

"And you're good at it. I'll appreciate you this year. I think Lindsey will be the most challenging with her severe and volatile behavior. Her mother has been frightened of her on several occasions and she has an older sister Irene whom they can't ever leave alone with her. Did you meet her mother Cindy?"

"Yes, but only for a minute. She was quite distracted."

"Yeah, that woman is on the verge of a breakdown herself. They've had Lindsey for three years but if they can't find a solution soon, they might give her up. What a waste of a life. I need to concentrate on her. No one has gotten through to her, so she's my particular challenge. And with you here, I can do that. Let's check her file."

Lindsey Hall: extremely manipulative. Out of control temper, exhibits rages with frequent regularity. Adopted at three years old after living in an orphanage about a year. Not much known about early life. Her acceptable behavior at adoption quickly began escalating out of control. Therapy has been in place for two years with limited success. Has been expelled by two grade schools and won't be accepted back without treatment and a special class attendance. Options are limited. Prognosis: One year at least in special needs class. Then reevaluated. Breakthrough must be found.

"Gosh," said Joanne, "that means she wasn't given up for adoption until she was two years old. She has a lot of memories and a lot of baggage apparently with that temper. Isn't there some information about her first few years?"

"No, doesn't seem like there is, at least nothing's in the file. That means, her parents, therapists and you and I are blindsided and just have to almost guess what her problems are. With Anita, Jimmy and Matthew, and to some extent

Peter, we know what happened and that helps a lot. It doesn't guarantee success but it sure helps. Lindsey is a closed book right now and her behavior is the only clue we'll get." April sat in her own thoughts for a moment as she looked at the next file.

Peter Lindsey: inside anger affecting his intelligence. Dropped off in a parking lot and abandoned at five years old. Didn't talk much at first but with the constant love of his adopted parents as well as good nutrition and therapy, he's showed improvement. Sporadically angry, causing extreme disruptions, but recently settled into more acceptable behavior. Prognosis: Special class for one year and reevaluation for regular school.

"Seems to me that Peter should be acting more like Lindsey," said Joanne. "Their background is similar. I mean, Johnny acts more like Lindsey and that makes sense but Peter, I don't know." April saw Joanne look confused as she read her copy of the file. And rightfully so.

"That's our biggest problem," continued April. "Human behavior has no rules. You can have the same or similar experience happen to ten different children and you'll get ten different outcomes. Our job would be so much easier if outcomes were similar. But this is where we have to evaluate the child and how they individually experience life. Not easy, but when we get it right, miracles happen."

"Yeah," said Joanne with renewed enthusiasm, "and that leaves Johnny. He'll be a handful though."

"True, Joanne, and, he can be your handful," related April with a wink. "I'll be busy with Lindsey. Here's how I see it. Peter, Matthew, Jimmy and Anita all need understanding, tender loving care, encouragement and time. Anything these children want to talk about that bothers them is a big plus. We will have to nudge them out into the open; I don't really see them creating any big disturbances in class. What we need to do with them is watch their reactions and when we see outward tears, or any type of upset, we talk to them about their feelings. While they are actually doing something physically or feeling a sensation is the time to work with them and get the best results. I've asked for one more aide, which I think we'll need. This will be a helper but very welcomed. However Johnny and Lindsey are the very outwardly angry children who are prone to rages. And during those times we can make progress in this class but we'll have our hands full with them. Do you think you're up to the challenge? Let's look at Johnny's file."

Johnny Patton: lived in foster homes and orphanages since birth. Two failed adoptions because they couldn't handle his angry behavior. Finally adopted again at five and a half years old. Very angry and hateful around other children. Outwardly mean and vindictive, but not usually physically abusive. No loving care as a baby, lack of being held and touched showed up as nasty behavior later on. With truly caring adoptive parents, his progress is impressive as he has developed a bond and found someone in the world who cares about him. With decent nutrition and therapy, he has begun to grow stronger and taller and although he still acts like somewhat of a bully, he's much closer to other normal children who exhibit this type of behavior during certain stages in their young lives. Prognosis: One year of special class should answer questions as to his further needs.

"Okay April, and you're here if I need advice, right?"

"Of course Joanne. He's a lovely child inside. He's so afraid to trust, let go and just like people. But he's learning."

"And you have Lindsey?"

"Yes I have Lindsey, and, at this time, I have no comment. She comes with no set of instructions but she's a child who desperately needs help."

April stood up and stretched. "Oh, look at the time!" she said, "Anyway, soon I want to try the first reading circle."

"That's always fun," said Joanne, and April noticed her looking up at the ceiling. "But I know, after the first few times that we get these kids in close proximity, they begin to relate somewhat. I've always thought you had a good idea there."

"Yeah, but the first few times are usually very chaotic. Yet, after forcing them to accept each other in physical closeness, in a way that little six and seven year olds can understand, that's the test. I love to see how they all grow through that. And of course, in public school they do have some round circle discussions and they have to be able to participate and behave properly."

During the second week, after the children had gotten to know each other a little, April invited them to sit in a circle up in the front of the classroom on the plush purple rug. Lindsey had a comment immediately.

"Do I have to join this reading circle thing?" Lindsey's tone of voice was rude accompanied by an irritated look on her face.

"Oh yes," answered April enthusiastically, ignoring Lindsey's obvious lack of interest. "We're all going to read together for a few minutes every day and then we'll play games and do other fun stuff. But first, let's read a story." April watched as Lindsey slowly and reluctantly got out of her seat at the back of the room where she felt safe and could see all of the activity in front of her with no one behind her. But April had to move her out of her comfort zone.

"Don't sit too close to Lindsey; she don't like nobody," said Johnny.

"You're the one I don't like," answered Lindsey as she sat down between Anita and Peter. Neither of them made any comment.

"Johnny, you have to apologize for pushing Matthew to the ground." Johnny looked shocked as he couldn't believe the teacher had seen him. But April didn't miss very much.

"I didn't do anything, ah, ah Ms. April. I didn't."

"Johnny, just say you're sorry. We'll wait." Since the other kids began to snicker, Johnny apologized quickly to get the attention off of him.

"Okay, good Johnny. What I want to do is have each of you take a turn reading. The one who's reading will sit in the center of the circle. I do want to mention that not everyone here is at the same grade level in reading. Some of you read better than others, so we must all be patient with each other, okay? Who wants to go first?" Anita volunteered and read fairly well although quite slowly, only pausing slightly at the beginning. April noticed that Johnny rolled his eyes to the ceiling but Lindsey sat still and patiently listened. Matthew, Jimmy and Peter were quiet as well.

Then April picked Lindsey who did very well, although her demeanor still showed that she didn't like being in close proximity with these other children and kept looking around between sentences. Next came Matthew who stuttered throughout his attempt. He knew the words but had trouble saying them. Johnny picked this moment to laugh and point at him. April stopped the session.

"One of the things we need to learn in this class is how it feels when you try your best and someone laughs at you. Yes, it's true that Matthew stutters somewhat, but he is improving and he did get through the exercise very well. We know you try very hard, Matthew and that's good. Johnny realizes that too, don't you Johnny?"

"Yeah, okay," said John unconvincingly.

"And Johnny doesn't like it when people laugh at him when he tries to do his best, do you Johnny?" Johnny became very quiet for a long minute as April just stared at him.

"Do I have to say I'm sorry again?"

"Only if you mean it, Johnny. Only if you realize that you hurt Matthew when he's trying very hard to improve. If you know that, then you can say you're sorry."

After a long pause Johnny said, "Okay, I'm sorry Matthew." This caused a few giggles in the circle which April accepted as childish humor.

"That's nice of you Johnny. Don't you think so, Matthew? It's good when you can apologize to someone you've hurt. Good job, Johnny." April saw Matthew smile at Johnny and the look on the faces of all the children said volumes about the confusion they had just witnessed. *Good,* thought April. *First of a thousand repetitions of this lesson.*

The next few months had many up and down episodes. The main purpose of special needs classes, as far as the lawmakers were concerned and the only reason it could be funded, was to help improve the children so that they could make the transition to regular school. Getting along with other children was at the top of the list, as well as listening to the teacher, learning to stay in their seats and not causing too many disruptions.

Other cooperative projects saw much improvement in the children's ability to get along. Getting to know each other and learning their weaknesses helped somewhat, but learning to help each other and to cooperate during projects went a long way too. Even Johnny was more cooperative and didn't laugh at other kids as much. He now realized that he didn't like it when others laughed at him, because it hurt. The other kids accepted him more now and stopped teasing him about being so little, which helped. There was some cooperation on good days, but worrisome behavior still existed quite often. However, April felt the children were improving and she still had almost seven months to go. Children would always fight and that was just a fact of life. But these children had to stay within normal behavior for their age group and April's job was helping them attain it.

# Chapter Two

On some days April got to speak with Lindsey in private moments. These conversations were very informative and insightful.

"I still think some of these kids are weird, Ms. April. Some are almost totally nuts, aren't they?" April noticed that Lindsey was spitting out her words very deliberately, a habit she'd picked up when she was upset.

"Each child here has specific problems, just like you," she answered.

"But we only have six kids here. Isn't that kind of small for a class? I know for sure that other classes have twelve kids. And one class I know for sure has fifteen kids in it. They go on field trips and sometimes they even go to the zoo. That's what I want."

"Okay, Lindsey, how many kids would you like in here?"

"At least ten. Yeah, ten kids would be just about right." April noticed that Lindsey was staring directly into her eyes, almost demanding an answer.

"So you want four more strange kids, as you call them, in my class. I'd need more help, wouldn't I?"

"Maybe the other kids don't have to be strange. What do you think of that?"

"I'm allowed six kids in this special class because I only have one assistant teacher and one aide. That's the decision made by the school board. Do you understand?"

"Oh," said Lindsey dragging out her word and April knew she didn't understand so she pressed on.

"Why do you think these kids are so strange, Lindsey?" This was an answer April really wanted to hear. Lindsey had very strong ideas and opinions that she never hesitated to express.

"I can't believe you even asked me that, Ms. April. Just look. Peter is seven and a half years old and he's in Grade 1 and he still can't tie his own shoes. Anita pees in her pants sometimes, right here in class. Imagine that at six years old. And Johnny is six years old but he looks like he's only three because he's so small. Jimmy and Matthew both have a lot of trouble talking and that really irritates me."

April waited as she could tell by Lindsey's fidgety behavior that she wasn't finished yet.

"Why do I have to be here? I can talk just fine. I've tied my own shoes for years now and I look normal. And I don't pea in my pants. Why did my mom and dad put me here?" As she finished April noticed that Lindsey's confusion and frustration had her close to tears.

"We need to help you deal with your anger. You get very mad at times and also you need to learn to get along better with other children before you can go back to regular school," was April's soft reply.

"That's dumb," replied Lindsey angrily, "I only get mad when people try to tell me what to do. I don't like that. If people don't tell me what to do, then I'm okay. It's simple. My parents are nicer to my older sister than to me and she's nine. But then, she's not adopted."

It was obvious to April that Lindsey's last remark slipped out accidentally and she stopped cold. Her eyes moved down to the floor quickly while she tried to control herself and the mistake that she thought she had just made. April was waiting when she finally had the nerve to peek upward into her teacher's face. As April saw anger spread across her face, Lindsey continued. "I can't understand why my other mom gave me away. But I know she didn't love me, you know. She just gave me away. That would make anybody mad, wouldn't it? Wouldn't it make you mad?"

"Yes, it would. I would certainly wonder why it happened and want to know the reason," said April looking at Lindsey who was looking everywhere else in the room to avoid April's eyes.

"I sort of have two moms and I don't like that. This mom tells me that I'm special, but I'm not special. And what happens if I do something that's not so special? Will they give me away too? I get real scared sometimes." The more irritated and angry Lindsey got, the softer, calmer and slower April would speak.

"I can understand that Lindsey. Maybe we can find another way for you to feel instead of afraid all of the time. What do you think, and look directly into my eyes when you tell me your answer, okay?" asked April since she knew Lindsey didn't have enough trust for eye contact and was trying to nudge her along. She saw Lindsey look into her eyes briefly more as a challenge and a defiant need to be in control.

"I don't know how else to feel. Really, two moms. I don't get it. Who'd give their kid away? Nobody would give away a good kid."

"I'm sure your other mom loved you too, just like this mom, but maybe she had problems and couldn't keep you."

"I'm like a throw-away kid. I am, you know." Then April saw Lindsey stop the conversation, get very shy and not say another word. This was her pattern. When she was finished talking, April couldn't get another word out of her no matter how hard she tried. It was just like she'd erased her feelings and they didn't exist any more, at least not consciously. She had built up a wall inside of herself and the wall only came back down if Lindsey made the decision.

After three months of class, the reading sessions were very gratifying for both April and Joanne. The children had gotten used to being in close proximity with each other and there were less fights to stop. They seemed to be inching their way closer to normality. Even Jimmy got over his nervousness to a great extent and volunteered to be the first one to read in a new book. Big step for him.

"I'm going to (pause) try my (pause) best." And so he began, reading slowly sometimes, other times moving on like any other child his age. He was doing a good job until he got totally stuck on a word.

"I don't know this one," he said.

"Me neither," said Matthew who was always the first one to try to help Jimmy.

"Anyone want to help?" asked Joanne and Johnny actually volunteered.

"Oh, Jimmy, that starts with the letter 'e', you know 'eeeee,' said Johnny trying to help him with the sound. And he walked him through the entire word.

"Oh yeah, I remember now, thanks," said Jimmy with a confused look on his face. "Yesterday, you made fun (pause) of me and that hurt (pause) but today you're helping me. (pause) How come?"

"I was in a bad mood yesterday. Sorry," said Johnny looking down at the floor.

"That's okay. You helped me today (pause) and you didn't laugh."

"No, I won't laugh, cause you're doing good Jimmy."

"Thanks Johnny, thanks a lot."

Matthew went into the circle with a hesitant attitude. He looked around rather nervously as he never felt comfortable reading.

"T-the c-cat in t-the h-h-hat."

Everyone wanted to help Matthew as he was a little more nervous but even he was gaining courage with a group of little ones who were not there to make fun of him anymore but usually more cooperative. Two days earlier, Johnny had made fun of Matthew, but then, as if he remembered, he apologized without being told. This was the new picture of the children – on a good day, of course. On a bad day, they were at each other. And that was okay. They were children but they were learning to cooperate and this was one step back to regular school. They looked forward to the reading sessions now and it was part of the day's activity. Even Lindsey seemed to have more patience with the slow and stuttering readers as she was able to occasionally give encouragement to Anita, Matthew and Jimmy. But mostly she still ignored Johnny.

"Good morning Lindsey," April said as she noticed her in the doorway to the classroom. "Are you coming in today?

Come in and take your seat, okay?" Lindsey always stopped at the doorway and looked around the room very deliberately and thoroughly. Her eye movement and body language said it all to April as she knew from that moment on Lindsey knew, at any moment of the day, everything that was going on in any corner of the room. It was the only way she felt safe.

One day Lindsey came in and just walked right through the doorway without pausing. This usually meant that she wanted her space and no one should disturb her.

"Leave me alone, Anita. Go back to your seat." Anita had gone back to talk to Lindsey and came back crying.

"No, I don't want to join you. Why would I? Go away," Lindsey said as she pushed Johnny and he hit her in the arm and April moved fast before a total fight broke out between them. The aides kept the other children busy as April went back to talk to Lindsey.

"What are you drawing?" asked April as she noticed Lindsey was working on white paper using black crayons only and the figures just loomed out at you. There was no reply.

"What's happening with you today?" she asked again. No reply. April waited a moment and then tried again.

"Why is your drawing so dark today?" Again, no response. So April waited. She just stood there in Lindsey's space and waited. After what seemed like an eternity Lindsey spoke in a very angry voice, "Move away. It's making me crazy."

"I'll be here until we can talk to each other. Yes, I will," replied April in her usual soft voice. The louder and angrier Lindsey became, the softer and calmer was April's tone of voice. No one spoke again for several minutes.

Eventually April asked, "Why are you so angry today?"

"I dunno," Lindsey replied with a pout, but that was all she said. April waited again.

"I dunno why I'm mad, but I am," she repeated this statement very slowly and very angrily. At this point, April noticed Lindsey was beginning to pound her fist on her desk.

"Were you angry when you woke up this morning?"

"Uh Huh. When I woke up, I felt wild." April knew Lindsey was irritated by the conversation and began to make a clucking sound after each sentence. And she kept pounding her fist harder on the desk.

"Did you have a bad dream?" April continued since she wasn't about to give up on her since she was answering, albeit in angry tones.

"No, I dunno; I don't remember," answered Lindsey adding more clucking sounds.

"You don't remember a bad dream or you don't remember dreaming at all? Which is it?" April noticed that as the conversation continued, Lindsey's fist pounding was letting up slightly. But she sighed in total irritation. "Too many questions," as April saw her lip curl up and heard a snarling sound.

"Yes I do. Do you remember dreaming?" April persisted.

"No, no bid deal. Happens all the time. I get mad at everybody and everything. Don't know why." This time Lindsey was furious. April couldn't decide if she was angry at herself or the situation. Her voice got very loud again and her fist pounding was frightful. It was evident that soon she would be in total uncontrollable rage.

"Do you want to stay angry like this?"

"No," she yelled, "I'm not stupid. Can't help being mad, except maybe sometimes. I'm angry and I'm scared." April had already witnessed one of Lindsey's rages that was considerably milder and more controllable but this one was serious so she signaled the aides to take the other children outside. She needed to protect Lindsey first from hurting herself and then use the opportunity as it presented itself to ease some of her deep inner pain.

Suddenly, Lindsey kicked her desk hard and her fist came down unbelievably strongly. She tried to bolt out of the room but was caught by April who immediately pulled her down to the floor and held her in a modified holding technique.

"Let me go, let me go." April heard sounds of growling amongst yelling and screaming as Lindsey tried to kick and punch her. If she could have managed it, there was no doubt that Lindsey would have bitten her teacher or inflicted some type of pain to match what she felt. She wiggled and turned her body around as much as she could but April had Lindsey's legs in a scissor-hold that limited her movements. She was able to hold her arms and upper body firm while Lindsey proceeded to struggle with all the power within her.

"Let me go. I hate you. I hate you!"

Despite the screams and nasty words, April's voice remained soft. Although Lindsey fought hard, April held on.

Talking very gently, April urged Lindsey to release the anger, to scream and yell if she wanted, which only angered Lindsey more at first. On and on the struggle went with Lindsey sure she could sneak away from the grip and with April just as sure she could hold on. A six-year old rage-filled child can have tremendous strength but April knew the holds involved and so far she was managing. It seemed like forever but she knew she couldn't loosen her grip for a second or she would be overpowered by a six-year old and would have lost a valuable moment. Her piecing screams in April's ears sounded like someone trying to escape the worst terror imaginable and mentally that is exactly what she was trying to do. She was trying to escape an inner prison that was like a torture chamber.

"Why are you doing this? Let me go. Let me go," screamed Lindsey more and more.

"I won't hurt you sweetie, but I want to help you let all that anger out. Keep yelling, get it out. Scream what you're mad about; it's okay."

Finally some of the words came out, "You're a terrible mother and I hate you. Why did you leave me?" she cried and yelled as April listened to more. "You left me by myself and I was scared. I was so scared. Why? Why did you leave me?"

"I love you sweetie. You're okay now. You're safe," said April very softly.

"I'm not safe. I didn't know nobody and I was scared. I hate being scared," as she heard Lindsey sobbing on and on. "Why did you leave me all by myself?"

April heard Lindsey repeating words more to herself than out loud, "Why? Why? Why? Why did you do that to me? Why didn't you want me? Why? Why?" April knew this child had kept that same question buried for a very long time, maybe even from herself. Very slowly the rage had settled but there was so much sobbing, deep sobbing that only the hardest of hearts would not feel. These sobs came from the buried pain, neglect, and questions that had gone unanswered. Lindsey was shaking now but she had started to relax a little in April's arms; she didn't struggle so much to get away but she kept on sobbing.

April looked up at the clock and found that approximately ten minutes had passed. It seemed so much longer. It took almost another five minutes for the intense sobbing to reduce into more calm tears that slowly, very slowly ended up in deep breaths with just the occasional sob.

"Do you feel calmer and safer now?" she asked.

Although Lindsey nodded her head up and down, her shoulders were still hunched up saying, I'm not sure.

So April held on. "Let me hold you just a little longer, okay sweetie?" she asked.

Lindsey, at this point, actually nudged her head deeper into her mentor's shoulder and made no effort to move. Being held close and seemingly enjoying it was a good moment for both of them. They stayed on the floor a few more minutes giving Lindsey more time.

"What does it feel like to be so angry? Can you tell me how it feels?" April asked.

Slow to respond, Lindsey finally said. "It's scary and it hurts a lot. Feels bad and ugly and I scream and yell because I dunno what to do."

April saw a tear escape from Lindsey's eyelid. She watched it slide downward on her face even though Lindsey tried hard to keep it from doing so.

"I feel dark inside. Dunno, but that's how I feel. I hate it. When I'm upset, I'm dark." Lindsey still cried intermittently at this point. "Don't want the other kids to see me cry. I'd hate that."

"Would it be so bad if the other children saw you cry? They cry a lot and even grownups cry sometimes." Knowing recess was almost over April signaled for the aides to keep the other children at the front of the classroom.

"Yes it would matter if they saw me cry. They can cry but I can't. I have to take care of myself." April saw that Lindsey was very agitated about this.

"That's a big job for a six year old. You're still a little girl and you need some grown up to help take care of you too, don't you think?"

"No, no. I only trust me. I have to take care of me."

"What about your mom and dad? Don't you trust them a little?"

"They're not my mom and dad." Lindsey answered angrily again, but in control. "This mom makes me mad most of the time. She's not really my mom and she might leave too. They all go away, you know."

"Why are you upset with this mom? Isn't she nice to you?"

"I dunno." Lindsey shrugged her shoulders again. "She's kind of nice to me sometimes, but not always 'cause sometimes she makes me go to my room."

"Oh, I see. Do you deserve that?"

"Maybe sometimes, but other times I just get mad and hate her and I dunno why. Nope, I dunno why. I scream and yell and then I feel better."

April knew that Lindsey was having a hard time trying to describe how she felt. She offered an idea. "Maybe we can use colors to describe how you feel inside. What do you

28

think?" She knew that children can picture colors easily in their mind. "Pink, blue, yellow and all the light colors are happy and fun, right? But brown, gray and black can be sad and very scary. Okay?"

"Okay."

April knew immediately that Lindsey liked that idea. "Mostly I feel black inside. Sometimes that's all, no light colors. Those are bad days. Sometimes though, I have a little bit of color like lilac and pink; they're my favorites and on those days I feel good. They don't come very often though. On pink days I can even have some fun, but some days are dark and black right away when I wake up and then I'm mad all day. I dunno why."

"Okay, Lindsey. Tell me, do you remember yesterday when we were singing all together in class and you said you liked it and I saw you smiling, what color was that inside?"

"Oh that was pretty much pink and even bright like a halo. I like to feel like that, but I don't very often."

"We'll have to find a way, together, to get you more pink and halo light colors inside and see what we can do to find out why you get the black so much. Can we work on this together you and I; what do you think?"

"Maybe, but I don't always want to talk."

"What color do you feel right now?"

"Not as black as when we started. I feel better now, how come? The dark shadow is still there but it sort of moved to the side."

April could tell that even Lindsey was surprised to hear her own explanation, yet that was exactly what she felt and she liked being able to describe it in a way that made more sense.

"So maybe talking about how you feel helps a little, especially if we talk about doing something positive, feeling good and experiencing great colors at the same time, right?"

She saw Lindsey's eyes get big with instant realization as she said, "Yes, maybe it does, especially when I talk to you."

The other children were beginning to wander around so Lindsey joined her group and participated quietly for the rest of the day. Some moments were better than others, but in the past when Lindsey was angry, it was an all day episode and she stayed totally by herself. But today, she mingled with the others and April was pleased.

Soon after this incident, a conversation with Lindsey's mother was revealing and necessary as the parents, teachers and therapists all had to be on the same page.

"You mean that she let you hold her during her tantrum? She would never allow me near her. I'm so surprised. Is that good?" said Cindy, whose voice had a sudden enthusiasm in it.

"First of all, she didn't **let** me hold her. It was a position that I'd forced on her. I've used it several times before, when I could manage it, on children who are so filled with rage that they can't think or even feel at the moment. Sometimes, it does make an inroad to starting to relieve some of the anger. And that's our goal for Lindsey. She must begin to release the anger inside of her, and she has lots of it. She must at least recognize what she's angry about, let it out and then we can talk about it. Whether it's good or not, we shall see in time. But it's a beginning."

"That's at least encouraging. We've had no encouragement at all with several therapists we took her to see. They would talk to her for a while and then some of them just referred us to other therapists, because they didn't know how to reach her."

"These children are hard to reach. They have built up a huge wall of protection around themselves. Talking alone usually doesn't work because they are very manipulative and clever liars. They believe they have to lie to survive, so that's not necessarily a negative trait; it's natural for them to want to protect themselves. I want to make this clear. Lindsey doesn't lie like other children do, and we know that all children lie at times. She feels she needs to lie to protect herself because she doesn't trust anyone."

"My husband and I knew that we hadn't built up any trust with her but we just didn't know what to do. It's so frustrating."

"Hang in there, Cindy. This call is to let you know that I made it through one of her rages, hopefully the beginning of something. I can't call it trust yet, but we did connect for a few moments. It all begins with one step. And it's still early in the year."

"What can we do at home? We'll do anything."

"Nothing any different than what you're doing now. We want to keep her routine at home the same or she'll be suspicious. I only wanted to give you slight encouragement, and it is very slight, but I'll need you to watch her and if you notice any change of behavior, just let me know. It will help me."

"Of course. We watch her carefully anyway."

"This is to be only between you and your husband. I believe your other daughter is about nine or ten, right?"

"Yes, she's ten and quite mature."

"That's fine but she's not to be aware of anything. That's very important. Okay? I'll keep in touch. We've got a very long way to go, but hopefully we've begun. I'll certainly keep you informed."

"I'm so glad we found you April? You're like a blessing. We didn't know what to do and we'd have done anything. Tell me, how long have you been doing this work? I know you're a teacher but also a psychologist, right?"

"I'm a special-needs teacher with a degree in child psychology. I'm glad I'm here for you. You know, it was a task to get this special needs program accredited and funded by the state. Even now they reassess us every year, so that we truly only exist on a yearly basis."

"But there is such a need for this type of class. It gives Lindsey and others like her an extra chance to make it."

"We think this class is very important and so far the state thinks so too. Our success rate has been pretty high."

"You have so much knowledge and impressive techniques with these children."

"My thesis at the university had been about giving the final chance to some of these children who had harm inflicted on them, through no fault of their own. I presented my paper to the state lawmakers and they saw the value of this program. And every year we've been renewed. I hope we're here to stay."

"I do too, April."

April had a slight feeling of satisfaction as she put down the phone. Cindy's voice was coming through with some hope and that was nice to hear. She'd hoped that she hadn't put too much importance on the recent action, because it would take a few more weeks to know if Lindsey related to her differently in school. In the past, this type of breakthrough had eventually led to an element of trust from the child, and with that in place, April could moved forward.

Checking with her assistant Joanne, April found that Johnny Patton was mellowing a little.

"Johnny seems much more manageable in class. He apologizes without being told and he seems to follow instructions quite easily. Of course, some days are tougher but I think he's doing very well."

"Yes I've noticed that, Joanne. He seems to love to apologize these days. I think I heard him say he was sorry at least five times yesterday. Hopefully this will even out and he doesn't continually overdo in the apology department. Better yet when he doesn't do the behavior that requires an apology. But seriously, he's still just a little child and of everyone in this class, I think he's gotten the idea in his mind that people will forgive you if you are really sorry. So he'll be able to build relationships. That's good."

"Have you noticed, April, that Johnny gets mad, a little, and even occasionally pouts, but I don't see the rage behavior much? I haven't seen him come close to a rage lately, have you?"

"No, I haven't and I was thinking of that last night. This little one is starting to behave in the acceptable patterns. Now he acts funny, instead of angry, most of the time. That's a much better choice. It was like he realized that he had more fun telling jokes and clowning around. It's a much better way to vent inner frustration. And he really can be funny. I like his improvement."

Time moved on in the special needs class and April felt that even with the improvement she had seen in Lindsey, there were other issues that Lindsey kept closed, even to her

33

teacher. But Lindsey liked to talk to her teacher and each time it happened April got new clues as to the inside pain of this child.

"How come you don't care if I talk about my first mom and dad?"

"Well, Lindsey, they're part of who you are. They gave you the beginning of your life and this mom and dad are continuing. Understand?" said April.

"Sort of. But how come they never want me to mention my first mom and dad? And you know what else? They don't want me to tell people I'm adopted?"

"I don't know. Have you asked them?"

"No, only a long time ago. I asked but they didn't like it; I could tell. They said they didn't know her and didn't know anything. I knew they didn't like it. I can tell, you know. And my sister Irene goes nuts every time I say I'm adopted."

"I don't know why your parents feel that way. I know others that feel that way too. But you can talk to me about your first mom, if you want."

"Sometimes I want to talk about her, you know. I like to pretend she's somewhere. I've told you how scared I get and if she wasn't somewhere, that would make me mad. I think sometimes that maybe I love her too but then she makes me mad."

"Do you remember anything about your first mom or dad?" asked April and she noticed a rather satisfied look on Lindsey's face. She was happy someone was acknowledging them to her.

"No, I don't," Lindsey said letting out a big sigh. "I wish I could remember something, you know. She was my mom."

"That's sad and that must hurt. How does that make you feel?"

"I feel sad. She's gone and sometimes I cry. But nobody knows." Then, April saw Lindsey's face light up as she continued, "Maybe you know a little."

"I understand how you want to keep them real in your mind. Your other mom and dad did exist. That's a fact. There was probably a good reason why they couldn't keep you but a lot of moms have to give up their babies. They don't want to but they want them to have a better life. That's a nice thing to do, isn't it?"

"Yep, I guess so. Do you think that's why my mom gave me away?"

"I think there's a good chance that's why she gave you away."

"Maybe, maybe that's why," said Lindsey but April noticed she had a satisfied look accompanying her final comment.

Lindsey still got confused thinking about her life. Ms. April didn't mind her mentioning her birth mom and dad. In fact, Lindsey felt she was very interested to hear her questions. Her mom and dad didn't like it at all. Lindsey remembered a few conversations she had with them.

"Lindsey, I've told you all I know over and over. I have never met with your birth mom, or dad for that matter. You'll just have to learn to forget about them. We're your family now and we love you," said her father and he seemed a little angry because she'd asked him before.

*But I can't forget and why should I?* Lindsey thought to herself. *I've got a right to know. Somebody knows something and someday I'll find out. People get very mad when I ask, but I don't care. I think they should tell me.*

One night when her parents thought she was asleep she heard them talking. "Lindsey hasn't mentioned being adopted for almost three months now. I think she's finally over it," said her mom hopefully

"Yes thank God. She must finally be adjusting to us. It's been rough. I'm glad it's finally over," said her dad in a tone that made Lindsey think that it had been some type of battle and they had finally won.

Lindsey wanted to scream at the top of her lungs, *"It's not over, I'll never forget. I'm not stupid, you know. I know you get mad at me so I don't talk to you anymore about my other mother. But I still have all the thoughts and all the why questions and someday, yes, someday, I'll find out. But for now I'll just have to wait. I know that you say you love me and I think maybe you do but I will never forget and if you think you had a rough time, well what about me? I hurt a lot, all the time deep inside of me where no one can see, and no one can hear and no one can feel, except me."*

Lindsey often cried into her pillow; that's the secret she had learned. She didn't want anyone to hear her because, if they did, the lectures and reprimands would start all over again. She believed they loved her and cared for her but they didn't like her to talk about the fact that she was adopted and they definitely didn't want her to talk about her other mom. They wanted her to forget. Lindsey knew she would never forget. Not tonight, not tomorrow, not next week or next year. She knew she wouldn't ever forget in her whole entire lifetime.

A few months later, Lindsey realized that she could wait her turn in class with more patience. At one point, she even let Anita skip ahead of her in line and didn't get angry about it. Once when Lindsey was taking her turn reading, she made a silly mistake, but instead of getting angry at herself and throwing her arms up in the air as she would have done before, she took a deep breath, waited a moment or two and tried again. She smiled at herself, realizing that, in the past, no one could have gotten her to continue reading and she knew why. Inside she would have been thinking, *"If only I could read better, maybe my mom wouldn't have given me away. I'm not a good girl."* This was always on her mind. It was behind her every action and behind every pause when she spoke. *Why didn't she love me? Why? Why? Maybe I wasn't a good baby, maybe I cried too much and too loud or maybe I was just too much trouble by being bad.* She couldn't stop wondering. Before she'd always had to wonder to herself only. But now, she could talk to Ms. April.

One time after patiently waiting to find teacher alone, Lindsey approached her for a talk. She had something on her mind and it was tough to talk about. Finally she started.

"Ms. April, I'm mixed up. Nobody knows what I feel like in here," said Lindsey with her hand over her heart. "I think you do, maybe a little, at least I think so, but you don't know either for sure, right?."

"That's very true Lindsey. I can listen and you can tell me things and then I can try to understand, but no one except you knows how you feel."

"That's right, you can't know. That's what I thought. How could anyone else know unless they were adopted too?"

"I would have to agree with that Lindsey. I think you have it right."

"People don't know about me. My mom and dad don't know – no one gave them away. It hurts a lot. They think I should just be happy because they adopted me and I get nice clothes and toys and stuff. And I do like my toys, but I always hear them say that I should just appreciate it. They don't say that to Irene, but then, she's not adopted." Lindsey paused for a moment to see Ms. April's reaction – as usual, she was interested. "Why do I still hurt? And why do I get mad at my mom a lot?"

"Lindsey, dear, I don't think you get upset as often anymore. And why do you think you get mad at your mom? I would like to hear you answer to that question."

"Well, sometimes I'm mad at both of them. I hate them both. But maybe it isn't this  mom I'm really mad at, know what I mean? I really want to love my first mom too, but it's hard because I hate her. I don't think she loved me. She makes me so wild because I dunno why she gave me away. I just want to know. If I was bad; I just want to know. But then maybe it wasn't my fault. But this mom and dad didn't give me away, at least not yet. So, maybe I'm lucky."

"They do love you and they're good to you."

"From now on, I'm going to be real quiet about my other mom. What do you think?"

"I wonder if you've given them a chance to understand your feelings. We could all talk together about the color of your feelings and then maybe they could begin to understand. How about that?"

"I dunno. I'm okay now. When I wake up with black shadows inside, now I'm not as scared of them and I can change them because you showed me. I know how. My mom and dad think I'm doing good so they're happy now. They really like you. I don't trust them as much as I trust you but I think they're okay and my sister Irene, she's okay as long as I don't talk about being given away because that makes her cranky. I know that she can't ever know about me and that's okay because I can always talk to you. Sometimes I even think you **know**."

"No, Lindsey. I don't know. No one can ever know exactly how you feel inside and you know why? Because only you had those things happen to you. I think you're a very strong little girl. It's not important that anyone else knows how you feel; it's just important that you can handle how you feel and you're doing good now."

Lindsey liked the way Ms. April sort of smiled when she looked at her.

"We don't have much time left this year, do we?" asked Lindsey.

"Well, just a little over a month. This year has gone by fast, hasn't it?"

"That makes me sad, Ms. April. Maybe I won't have to move on but I can stay with you for another year?"

"Don't you think that you're doing good? We're all proud of the success you've had this year. And remember how much you loved public school?"

"But I like this class better. I can talk to you. You let me talk about my birth mom and dad. You said it was okay to think about them and have my own special thoughts about them."

"Yes I think it's okay for you to do that. But Lindsey, you can do that if you're in public school."

"I know. I know. But it just won't be the same," said Lindsey very sadly.

"Remember we talked about moving on and life would have more fun things for you to do. You will be learning many new things and making new friends. Life changes."

"I wish I could stay with you."

"Well, we'll keep in touch and I'll see you sometimes. And then I'll want to know that you're doing great and you can tell me about everything new that you've done, Okay?"

Lindsey just looked at her teacher and said, "But it won't be the same. It'll never be the same." And she turned and walked slowly out of the room.

Most of the children had done well in this special class. Peter was going on to regular school and his power of concentration was much better. He tied his shoes easily. Johnny had done well, and grew more than two and a half inches. He was still small but catching up to his peers. Girls were still not his favorite friends, but he could be nice to them, most of the time. Matthew and Jimmy had straightened out their speech so much that it was only occasionally that anyone could detect a slur or a pause. Anita was going to need more time. She had progressed and her anger had lessened but she was not yet ready for regular school. She still had accidents in class but they were less frequent and it was thought that one more year of special school would be all that was necessary. And Lindsey was moving on to Grade 2 in public school.

For the last day of school, Lindsey's mom had helped her pick out a card for her teacher. It had an angel with a halo and wings and a message that said, "*I understand now, Thanks to you.*"

"Well, I have something for you too." First was a card with a sweet little girl on the front and nice words inside that said, "*To my little Lindsey, a very bright little girl, who never quits but just keeps on trying. You'll be a big success in your life because you are now after this wonderful year you gave me. Love, Ms. April.*" And not only that, but Ms. April had written her two telephone numbers on the card so that

40

Lindsey could talk to her anytime she felt that she needed reassurance. When she saw tears beginning in Lindsey's eyes, April wanted to give her reassurance and said, "I'll always be your friend and always available to you."

Lindsey had come to terms with being adopted, and although she didn't like the fact that her birth mom had given her away, she did feel fortunate that she had another mom who was with her now. She wasn't yet totally convinced that this new mom and dad would always be there for her, because she thought they might leave too. But all through this year, Ms. April reminded Lindsey that her parents were still there and that they cared about her. And she always had Ms. April.

"I know you're there for me, Ms. April; I know you understand and you'll always be around somewhere, but it won't be the same. I won't see you every day and I won't be able to save my questions for you every day. That makes me so sad."

"Life changes every day and people change too. You're going to change a lot, Lindsey in the next few years, and grow taller and smarter. You've changed a lot inside just this year alone so before long, you'll depend on yourself more than on me."

April needed to remind Lindsey of one more thing. "You know that you're a strong little girl who's getting stronger every day. You can depend on yourself a lot now. You can even be the one who will help your mom and dad to understand. They try, you know, but they need your help." April meant to throw this challenge to Lindsey who was quite capable of handling it.

And Lindsey took the bait but with a new twist. "Maybe I can help them understand. And they can help others to understand. But when I get confused and scared, who'll help me understand? Can I always call you.?"

"Yes, oh yes, you can always call me and I expect to hear from you. I understand because that's what my study has been. I studied hard in school for many years to learn to understand little girls like you and my job is to help you and to help your parents understand too."

"That's a real nice job you have. I want the same job when I grow up," said Lindsey.

April noticed her get very quiet after that and although her eyes were still on the verge of tears, she fought them back and joined in with the rest of the children.

Just before she walked out the door with her mom, she paused and ran back to Ms. April and gave her a big final hug and said, "I love you in a special way." April replied staring directly into her eyes, "I love you in the same special way. We understand, don't we?" And with that Lindsey turned slowly and reluctantly and walked out the door with her mom without looking back, knowing that this part of her life was gone forever and wouldn't ever come back again.

# Chapter Three

Cindy and Clarence Hall were excited with the progress Lindsey had made in Ms. April's class. It was slow progress at best, but solid, showing new positive differences.

"You know Cindy, when I look back over the last three years since we got Lindsey, I think only the first few months were relatively calm and free from intense anger and control from her."

Cindy smiled as she thought about the first few weeks. "Yeah, when she first got her, she had a rather wide-eyed wistful attitude, amazed at all of the comforts and I know she liked our home. Remember how she loved having her own room."

"Right and by the third day she came in with three sweaters that belonged to Irene," laughed Clarence. "She had helped herself to some of Irene's clothes which threw Irene into a fit."

"Those were only the little problems. She learned very quickly what was hers and what belonged to Irene or anyone else in the house and how these two facts didn't leave room for negotiations." Both laughed in remembrance.

Clarence stated. "But she was really bright for a three-year old. She knew how to negotiate and bargain. I'm not sure if being moved around from one home to another

43

prepared her for this, but she learned to stand strong for what she wanted, even from the beginning."

"You know Clar, I think that Irene was the one whose life was impacted the most and she wasn't happy with Lindsey at all. For being only three years older, she felt that her younger sister got away with a lot of stuff. It was like we excused her from things because she was adopted, and maybe we did. Anyway, Irene thought Lindsey was a brat."

"Lindsey was very manipulative, every day."

"More like every hour," Cindy added. "There was always something occurring that bordered on catastrophe. And her temper was rather frightening. I don't know what we'd have done if we hadn't found April Munson and that special needs class. Her anger has calmed down immensely at home and at school. Her trial into Grade 2 proved successful and Grade 3 has gone pretty well."

Taking a deep breath, Clar said, "It's good to relax in your own home." Clarence believed the conversation was over and went back to reading his paper. Cindy relaxed in her newfound confidence that life was moving on well for her family. They hadn't taken the seminars and classes for parents that April had suggested, but felt they could do that in the future if the situation arose.

And the Hall home was much more calm and relaxing and fun all during the time that Lindsey remained in Grade 3 and into Grade 4. They kept an eye on her behavior and she was passing the test. There were no reports of behavior problems at school. Grade 5 brought on a few disturbances but not the outside ordinary limits of a ten year old. However, some anger was being expressed by Lindsey at home and Irene began complaining again of unpleasant conduct by Lindsey. This progression seemed so slow that as it continued inching its way into more severe problems, it was like it struck again overnight. But it hadn't. It had remained buried and then exploded as it was destined to do. By the end of the first month of Grade 6, they were summoned to the school. Lindsey's anger problems were serious again at school and she was being written up on bad reports and disciplined with regularity. Within two weeks of their first visit another emergency meeting was called with the principal and one of her teachers for the next day.

"I'm close to giving up, Cindy. We've got nowhere to go and no one knows for sure what to do." Clarence's eyes belied his composure as their redness told of his inner anguish.

"I can't take it anymore and I don't know either." Cindy remembered her own evenings crying, upset and on the computer looking for answers. She didn't like to see Clarence so upset. Yet there were no answers. What should they do? What could they do?

"Maybe we should admit defeat and send her back, if we can. I mean, what are we supposed to do?" said Clar in his continual frustrated attempt to make sense out of a senseless position. "This kid has definite mental problems. She just acts crazy and the time will come when we just have to give up because we can't help her."

Cindy continued, "I think I'm going crazy. She just hates us so much no matter what we try to do. Why didn't someone warn us how it would be?"

"Maybe they didn't know."

"Or didn't want to tell us." Clar was looking into space and winced at the thought crossing his mind. He looked at Cindy suddenly and neither one liked the thought crossing their minds. Did these social workers and adoption agencies actually know the trouble ahead for adoptive parents and not say a word?

"They would have told us, or at least warned us, wouldn't you think?"

"I tell you Cindy, this guy at work told me about a couple who sent back two little girls they'd adopted. They'd had them about two years and they were just acting crazy and uncontrollable. His wife had a complete breakdown. I guess it was an awful situation."

"Really, they did it. They sent them back?"

"Yeah, the girls were about eight years old when they adopted them and sent them back at ten years old. They just couldn't take it anymore."

"Kinda sad though. For the parents true, but for the kids, another rejection which probably makes them even worse."

"Why don't they match up parents and kids better?" asked Cindy. "But then again, how could they have known who to match Lindsey with?"

"They must have known something about this behavior. If only we had known anything at al!"

"Remember the parent support group we heard about from Diane. She said that most of the parents in that group have very little children, under five years old. She said that those parents are in total shock regarding the behavior of these little children."

"Something is wrong with this system of adoption. Why didn't they tell us? I don't know if I would have agreed to all of this?"

"I know Clar that I'm mentally whipped and emotionally I'm not doing any better. There aren't any answers for us and no answers for Lindsey." Cindy was shedding tears again. They were both at the end of their emotional road. What were they going to do? What was left for them to try?

The next visit with the principal was critical. Mrs. Dixon began the discussion. "You have to do something with your child, possibly anger management classes. Anything sets her off, not just the usual childhood problems but the slightest comment. And she's not a very happy child. Some days when she first walks into the classroom, you know there will be trouble. She needs help. We can't give it to her here. And we can't have her disrupting everything. I think we're going to have to suspend her until you find a solution. I'm sorry, I know this is hard for you, but this is her absolute last chance."

"Can you give us a week? We'll try to find someone. We'll do anything but we're at the end too and don't know which way to turn." Mrs. Dixon saw a woman on the verge of tears and felt for her, but she had a school to operate. "We've tried all we can think of. She's the same way at home. All this anger. Yet, she has to go to school. Don't you know anyone that can help us, Mrs. Dixon?"

"Settle down, Cindy, relax a moment," said Clar as he turned anxiously to the principal. "My wife is at the breaking point and this is affecting Irene too. We've been to so many therapists...." Suddenly Clar's face lit up with an idea. "Hon, April – we've got to find that April teacher, remember, what was her last name?"

"Munson," said Cindy perking up a bit, "yeah, April Munson."

With that Clar turned to Mrs. Dixon and told her about the special Grade I class and how it had really helped her. It was only for one year but even after all the therapists had failed, April had made a breakthrough. Cindy's expression changed too from despair to definite hope and this change was not lost on Mrs. Dixon.

"Yes, she was great with Lindsey when no one else could get to her. Why didn't we think of her before?" They would definitely call her today and see what they could set up.

Mrs. Dixon decided to give the Halls one week, but during that time Lindsey would be separated from her usual class and given only study hall if her behavior got irrational again.

April Munson had moved around a little, but they finally found her through the education community. Concerned by the panicky phone call detailing Lindsey's progress, or rather her recent lack of progress, she accepted an appointment within two days. She saw two very worried parents come into her office and try to settle down for a discussion.

"So the road has been rough for Lindsey. Okay, okay. But let's back up a bit. Where was she at after our class in Grade I? I talked to you about six months after and all was well. When did it start again.?"

"It didn't start all at once, at least not that we noticed. It was slow to begin with," said Cindy.

"She started having those severe temper tantrums and talked about dark shadows and stuff; it didn't make much sense to us," Clarence added.

"Yes I remember those very well. We'd found a way to help her with that. Didn't those classes help you out at all?" asked April.

"Honestly April, we must admit we didn't take them," admitted Clar. "She was so good after your class. She acted fine, just as good as Irene and we thought all would be okay. We know now that things did not turn out fine."

"Yes, well, it's probably not too late. These classes will help you understand how Lindsey thinks and where she's coming from. She doesn't see the world as you and I do. She sees the world from the viewpoint of distrust. She really doesn't trust at all. I think she was learning to trust a little back in Grade I and hopefully we can get her back there. You may see some similarities in your daughters on the outside but in their emotions and relationships to the world, they're miles apart."

"They're both just little girls, how can they be so different? They are both loved and cared for the same. We give them both a lot of attention and they're both in soccer and swimming and lots of other activities. What more can we do?" Cindy felt they were following the rules for parents.

"Irene's your birth daughter. She's always had that security. She sees the world as safe, loving and she can trust it. You taught her that. Lindsey can't see the world the same way. Her birth mother gave her away. Can you imagine how that must feel? She'll probably never totally trust that you won't give her away sometime in the future. Also, love is a little in reverse for her. Her birth mom gave her away, I'll come back to that a lot. That will never leave her mind so to her love is painful. People say they love you but they don't mean it and that hurts. Understand?"

"So she doesn't believe we love her?" Cindy asked.

"Probably not but it's more than that. She associates love with pain. My mom said she loved me but she gave me away. It hurt that she gave me away. Therefore, love must be painful. That's our biggest worry that she associates love with pain. So you can do a lot of nice things for her and she might like it and even allow herself to enjoy it, but to her that

49

can't be love. It's not painful. Get it? Don't worry. It's a tough concept and we'll keep at it."

Clar and Cindy just sat listening in disbelief at what they were being told. They felt that Lindsey was their daughter now. They'd had her for eight years and felt that she never thought about being adopted anymore. After all, she never mentioned it. During her first year, she used to ask a lot of questions about her mom and her other life but soon she stopped asking. The Halls thought that was a good sign. They felt all of the early memories were now gone and she had adjusted to her new life.

"Are you sure, April?" asked Cindy, "Because Lindsey never mentions being adopted, or her other mom. Why, I believe it's been several years now. We thought that was good."

"Cindy, she has a birth mom who gave her away. Probably most of her conscious memories have been gone for quite a while, but the deep memories will always be there and will color all of her thinking and anything she does."

"Wow," said Cindy, "we thought we'd done so well by making her forget."

"Lindsey will never forget. Who could? Could you? Could anyone? She was given away and doesn't know why. It makes her feel less valuable than others. And she's not alone. Most adoptees think this way."

"We just wanted her to be our daughter," said Clar.

"She is your daughter but she comes with a history and she'll always have a history. You can't take that away from her."

"Then we caused this anger?" said Cindy thoughtfully, "We thought we were helping."

"You didn't cause this anger. It was always there but we all have to work together to help Lindsey get it under control again and keep it under control."

"So how are we supposed to learn all this stuff? You're the analyst," said Clar in a frustrated tone.

April just smiled and waited.

"Oh yea, those classes, Sorry," he acknowledged with a touch of embarrassment.

"That's okay. Most parents don't love the idea of taking classes on how to raise their kids. They think it's just common sense. But it's so much more for some adopted children. It's a complex world for these kids and they need special help."

"We see what you mean."

"I'd like to give you an example of how Lindsey thinks. Maybe an example would be the best way to help you understand how clever these children are and to what lengths they will go to be in control. Control to them is so important. If they can control a situation, they won't be hurt again, they believe. That's how they think. Remember when we talked about how other therapists couldn't get through to her, even as young as six years old. I'm going to role model through how a session probably went back then, especially when the therapist saw her alone. She's very smart and very manipulative. It probably went something like this. I'll assume a male therapist"

> "Well, Lindsey, I understand that you're having some serious problems," the therapist began.
> "That's why my mom brought me here. But I'm okay."
> "Your mom tells me that you get very angry. Is that true?"

"No, I don't get angry. But I want my way," answered Lindsey.

"Don't you think you're too young to always get your way?" he asked.

"How old should I be?" asked Lindsey. She thought, *I'm happy that my mother is out in the waiting room. I don't have to tell the truth because this therapist will never know if I'm lying. I'm so happy that he made my mom wait outside.*

"How old do you think you should be?" asked the doctor.

"I get sad and afraid when they make me do things I don't want to do. Honestly, I get very afraid." Lindsey decided, *I'll put on a very sad face that I think will make this doctor feel sorry for me. I'm was right; I knew it. He'll soon forget about the age thing. I know what to do.*

"Your parents shouldn't make you afraid. I'm sure they don't mean to do that." The therapist by this time is very concerned.

"I don't know what they mean to do, but they scare me a lot." Lindsey thought to herself, *I think he needs to see me very upset now so that's what I'll do. I'm going to win this game.*

"How do they scare you Lindsey?" Lindsey had noticed that if she talked softer the doctor would lean forward toward her so he could hear her better, and then she knew she was in control. That made her happy but she couldn't look happy. She still had to play sad and unhappy right now.

"They like my sister Irene the best. But Irene isn't adopted, you know. And Irene doesn't like me at all. They always favor Irene." Lindsey thought *this would be a good time to use the tears and she did.*

"Now don't cry. I'll talk to your mom about making sure that they're just as nice to you as they are to Irene. Okay? Do you go to kindergarten yet?"

"Maybe next year, if I act better. They don't think I act good enough to go this year. I try to be real good, but they say it's not good enough." Lindsey would play every card in the deck for this doctor and she thought, *This is fun to watch him feel sorry for me. It's so easy to fool him; I think it's funny.*

"Okay, would you like to try to go to kindergarten this year?" Now Lindsey knew she had won over the doctor. He was totally on her side. This game was more fun than she thought.

"No, I'll be glad to wait. I don't want to upset my mom or dad. I can wait. Maybe by next year I'll learn how to act better and then they'll like me better." Lindsey is happy the therapist is believing her..

"I'm going to talk to your mommy now. Some kids your age go to kindergarten or to pre-kindergarten and that might be good for you. Would you like me to try to set that up for you?" He was really trying to make her feel better. She didn't think her mom was going to be happy. But making her mom unhappy was part of the game.

"Okay," and Lindsey managed to give the doctor a weak smile on the way out.

"Do you see where I'm going with this? Lindsey was in control and I'm sure Lindsey was having fun controlling those situations. I don't blame the therapists because these children are very clever. You know, all children lie and are manipulative at times. To a degree, that's normal. Let's say your other child wants to see if she can get extra allowance money out of you or not have you find out she misbehaved in school; she'll put on the act. That's what normal kids might do. But to these children it's not a game; it's their survival and they are very, very good."

"I know that these therapists didn't even get a glimpse

53

of what we're seeing at home. And that was a big worry to us. We were totally the bad parents to them, not helping this poor little victim. Now, that's not to say that we couldn't improve as parents, because that's what we wanted to learn. How could we help this child."

"And Lindsey was a totally different child. She presented to the therapists exactly what she wanted them to see," continued April. "And that wasn't her angry, and painful self. Remember, you have a special needs child. She was almost three years old when you got her and she was moved around a few times before then. She has some problems to deal with but we'll discuss this further in time. But for today, you have an idea about Lindsey. You say the school's ready to reject her for a special needs class?"

"We probably will have to switch her again." said Cindy taking a deep sigh.

"I'd hate to see that happen," said April. "What school does she attend?"

"Howe Elementary in Janesville. She's in Grade 6."

"Oh, I didn't know you had moved. When was that?"

"It's been almost two years." said Cindy sending a confirming glance to Clar.

"Interesting. And her behavior got worse around that time?" asked April.

"Why yes, I think that's when it started again" confirmed Clar.

"Might be a connection; might not. But the good news is that I've begun working with some schools. I spend an afternoon or more a week to counsel and guide some teachers and children. Howe is on my list and I will be there starting sometime next month."

Clar and Cindy were thrilled. Lindsey loved Ms. April, as she called her, and that should really help. There was an element of hope returning.

"But I want to see Lindsey as soon as possible. Tomorrow sometime, okay?"

"Yeah, great. We'll get her here."

"Good. I need to see where she's at right now and get her back on track."

"Do you think you can?" asked Cindy anxiously.

"That's up to Lindsey, but she did it before. I'll want to see her alone tomorrow but I want to see you both again, sometime after Lindsey and I've talked a few times."

The next day found Lindsey walking into April's office. April was surprised how much she had grown and how, despite a real attempt on her part, some hair still escaped and managed to find its way into her eyes. Lindsey seemed happy to see her yet there was no hug, no physical contact at all.

"Good to see you. Lindsey. You've certainly have grown in five years. You're getting to be such a young lady and a very pretty one at that." April was trying to begin the conversation on a light note but Lindsey remained very superficial.

She smiled and said she was genuinely happy to see Ms. April but it wasn't the same. There was no doubt about that. April could tell immediately by her posture and demeanor that Lindsey had regressed. After the usual nice questions, April began.

"Tell me what's happened to you? You didn't call me very much after the first three months."

"I'm sure you already know all about me. Probably everyone's told you how bad I am now anyway." Although Lindsey exhibited some anger in her statement, April was more concerned that she didn't seem to care about her behavior.

"I have heard some stories about you, but I'd like you to tell me now." April had to keep the conversation honest.

"It won't matter. Nobody likes me; they all hate me. And I don't care."

April realized that Lindsey was sitting in a similar position that she had when she first entered her special needs class. The only difference today was that she hadn't been able to choose a seat in the back of the room. Otherwise, Lindsey had seemingly reverted back to the same angry child she was before. Hopefully, thought April, something could be salvaged.

"I heard you had some problems at school." This was a simple statement and April waited for her reaction.

"Well, ya. They don't like me and I don't care. Those girls wish I weren't even in their class so maybe I won't be."

"Is that why you act bad, so you can change classes?"

"Maybe. Well no, no, that's not it. Remember when we talked about the dark shadows in me, well, they've been back for a while now and I can't stop them." April saw Lindsey spitting out her words again as she did when she was a six year old.

"Did you remember to ..."

"Yeah, I remember switching something light for something dark but it doesn't work anymore. It doesn't work like it did before." Lindsey was really sulking now.

"Why do you think that is, Lindsey?"

"You helped me and on a real bad day you taught me how to make the switch, but then things got so dark so fast and so many times that I just couldn't do it. It's so hard. You probably hate me too."

"No, I don't hate you Lindsey. I could never hate you."

"Yeah, right. You're just saying that. Everybody hates me."

"Why do you think I would hate you Lindsey?"

"Cause I do."

"Have I ever lied to you, Lindsey?"

"Well no, but you can't like me anymore."

"Why not?"

"Cause I'm bad. I'm bad at school and I'm bad at home and you don't like bad."

"What do I like Lindsey?"

"You liked me when I acted better and I tried but then you weren't there to help me. You left me, Ms. April and I needed you. You left me and it made me mad."

"I didn't leave you, Lindsey. We did talk on the phone at first, didn't we?"

"That's not the same, not the same at all," and with that

Lindsey pounded her fist on the arm of her chair. April thought she must have hurt herself since she pounded so hard, but her inner rage and pain was so deep again that her outer pain didn't register. Lindsey still pounded her fists when her fears became scary.

"I didn't leave you, Lindsey, but the class was over and you had to move on to regular school because you had really done so well."

"Anita stayed with you. Remember, you let Anita stay for another year."

"She wasn't ready to go to regular school, you know that. But you were. Let's talk about what happened."

"Maybe I wasn't ready either. You thought I was ready but I wasn't really ready and look what happened. I think you made a mistake with me."

"Lindsey, you were okay that summer. Remember you called me and told me about your trip to Disney World?"

She saw Lindsey smile remembering a fun trip. "Yeah, that was fun."

"How was Grade 2?" "Okay." "No problems?" asked April.

"Not really," Lindsey answered.

"How about Grade 3?"

"It was okay too," answered Lindsey very unenthusiastically.

"Just okay?" asked April.

"Yeah," was her blunt answer.

April was having trouble dragging much out of Lindsey. The trust between them was gone and she wasn't talking much. She had to try something else.

"How about Grade 6?"

Lindsey shot April a very quick, angry glance that could have bounced off all four walls. Her lips quivered and her jaw line reacted.

"Awful, I hate it and everybody in it." Lindsey changed her position to one of pouting.

"Gee that's a lot of hate you've got. What about Grade 5?"

"Not much better. Same. I didn't like it."

April had another question. "What or who do you like right now, Lindsey? Just tell me what or who you enjoy, right now?" With that said April waited and it did take a few moments before Lindsey spoke.

"Probably only Muffy."

April asked, "Muffy?" "Who is Muffy?" she asked.

"Our dog. She always listens to me and she don't get mad. Everybody else gets mad at me. But Muffy is my friend."

"Oh, I see." Well, there was one place that Lindsey felt safe. She could trust the dog. She could love the dog. It was a beginning and Lindsey had let slip a very important idea. The dog didn't get mad at her. That was a thought to hold onto.

"How about your mom and dad? How do you get along with them?"

Lindsey just shrugged her shoulders, looked down at the floor and didn't give much reaction one way or the other.

"How about mom?" No response. "How about dad?" No response. "How about your sister Irene?" Lindsey shot her another one of those glances.

"You don't like your sister?" she asked.

"She thinks she knows it all because she's older but she don't. She only thinks she does," said Lindsey frowning.

"Let's talk about the color of your anger. What color is it at home?" asked April.

"What's with this color? It won't work anymore. It's always black. It never changes and it's there when I wake up and it's there when I go to sleep. It just won't go away anymore." Lindsey expressed a deep sigh when her statement was over.

"I see," was all April said.

"It's like a big black hole just waiting for me to trip and fall into. I get scared and it makes me real mad." Lindsey almost let some tears escape when she was talking about the black hole and April began realizing how deep her pain had become.

"And you left me, Ms. April, in the middle of all this, you left me."

Why didn't you call me?"

"Cause you left me and I didn't have anyone who understood. You were the only one who understood. Mom and dad and Irene, I don't know if they even try or not, but they just don't get it like you did. I'm different than they are. They just don't know." She stopped for a moment. Then she asked, "Are you going to leave me again?"

"No, and I didn't leave you before," she reminded Lindsey. "Actually I'm going to be around a lot. Starting next month, I'm going to be spending time at Howe School so I'll be seeing you there."

"Really?" There was a very strong reaction from Lindsey after this comment.

"Yes, I am. I will be setting up classes and sessions."

"Like before, I can be in your class?"

"I'll have to see how you are doing, but I will be seeing you and I'll be available to you. How does that sound?" April watched Lindsey's physical body sit up in a more positive position. She was remembering how happy she'd been in April's class and an unspoken bond seemed to be returning.

The next few days found April getting some facts and information together for the parents. There were two sides to this issue that had to be addressed. Cindy Hall, especially, was in a very delicate emotional condition right now. She was on the verge of collapse, physical, mental or both. She had only survived this long with the help on her husband, who was also showing the end of his resistance. Living with special needs children could be a constant nightmare and the world didn't realize how much anguish the parents suffered. They lived with rage-filled children every day, usually without preparation or understanding. No wonder some of them gave up and sent the children back. Some marriages collapsed under the strain. "I feel like I'm on a roller coaster ride with Lindsey's emotions, anger and rage. I'm trying to love a child who doesn't know how to accept my love. Most of our friends and neighbors won't let their children play with Lindsey anymore." These were the usual comments from Cindy and common among other parents. And if the parents couldn't handle it, Lindsey would get moved again and who knows how another rejection and abandonment would affect her. Some parents could hang on to the end, but many could not.

Hope had such a strange effect on people. Clar and Cindy carried it in their daily lives and brought it home in their family that desperately needed something to build on. April had diagnosed Lindsey with RAD (Reactive Attachment Disorder). This is a recognized mental condition where the individual doesn't trust and has trouble forming close relationships. Many adopted children fall into this category as well as foster children and even some children living with their birth families. There are many causes for this disorder and several methods to make repairs. However, when teachers, respite workers, therapists and parents all worked together, then a powerful group could help these children heal.

Within two weeks, April had a schedule of meetings set up for Lindsey. Every other day for the first month, she met with Lindsey for half an hour sometime in the morning at school. If she had a problem, she would stop in anytime before any detention or meeting with the principal. And Lindsey would have another meeting for one hour away from school every week while deemed necessary.

"Good morning Lindsey," said April on the first meeting at school since they began.

"Good morning, Ms. April."

"Okay, in these morning meetings we only have half an hour so if anything is bothering you, let's get to it quickly. Okay? Anything special on your mind?"

"Yes, but it doesn't have anything to do with school. Is

that okay?" said Lindsey staring at Ms. April hoping she could talk about anything that bothered her.

"That's fine. But first, how are you inside today? Dark or light?

"Not nearly as dark as usual. But I think it's because you're here. I've always felt better when you were around."

"Okay, and that's good. I'm glad you feel better." April was not real concerned about her dependency at this time. With the entire team working together the time would come when Lindsey could depend on herself. And when she couldn't, the future would find her calling April or any other appropriate person. "What's on your mind?"

"Well, I feel like I'm going to burst sometimes but now you're here and I can say that I dreamt about my birth mom last week for the second time in two months. You know I still can't mention anything to my mom and dad about her but I needed to tell someone. I was at a party and she was there. I couldn't really see her face and I'm not sure if she was with me or not but she did say 'Hi Lindsey' to me and she smiled nice. Isn't that good?"

"Yes, it looks like it made you feel good?"

"It makes me feel that she thinks about me sometimes wherever she is. I like that."

"Lindsey, I'm sure she does think about you. Let's talk about your mom and dad. Together we could talk to them and I'm sure they would understand how you need to talk about your mom now and then. Would you like to try?"

"I don't think so. So many times if I just hinted about her, everyone would get upset. Irene would go nuts too. So I don't care. Maybe they can't understand. Maybe they would try, but they just can't. And it's okay. I just need to make her real to me and I do that by talking to someone about her. And you always listen. That's really all I need right now."

"Okay, then you're okay with that. But I'd like you to think about it. We could maybe talk to them sometime in the future if you like."

"I don't think so but if I change my mind, I'll let you know."

"Any problems at school, classes, homework or anything else?"

"No. The kids don't like me very much but I've been acting mad a lot. Because I was mad a lot. Now I feel a little better. It just makes a big difference having someone to talk to that understands. And I know you understand."

"I don't understand everything"

"That's okay, at least you listen. Maybe that's all I need. I know that nobody can go back and fix things for me, but it makes me feel better when you listen."

"I'm glad you feel better. What about the girls in your classes."

"Some don't like me because I get in trouble and they think if they talk to me they will get in trouble too. So I kind of stay by myself. But some are nice and smile at me. So they don't all hate me. Honestly, Ms. April I can't really blame them. Some work hard and want to do good in school. And they do think I'm a troublemaker."

"Maybe you'll be able to change that in time. What do you think?"

"I want to try. I just hope I can stay in control, know what I mean?"

"Remember, Lindsey, for the next few months you have permission to leave the classroom, with permission, don't forget to get permission, and you can come and talk to me. This is only on a short terms basis but I think you're doing better already."

"Yeah I am. Guess I'd better get back now. Can I give you a hug? I've missed our hugs a lot." And with that Lindsey came around and gave April a hug. And as she turned to leave she said, "Seems more like old times to me. Bye."

On the parents' side, Cindy and Clar were to take the parenting classes with no shame. These gave instructions on the special and unique problems of some adopted children. They had to learn what was happening inside of Lindsey, her way of thinking and her view of the world that was so different from Irene and themselves.

When they arrived at the first basic lecture, Cindy and Clarence agreed they were there to learn and do whatever they could to help their family. They didn't know what to expect but they were very hopeful and happy to get some pointers to help their desperate situation.

The speaker came out and after a few polite formalities got to the subject matter strongly and quickly.

"You are here today, parents, because your lives are out of control and you have tried everything. You are at the end of the trail, so to speak, and are looking for help. Many of you have already looked into the possibility of returning your adopted or foster child and some of you here are having just as much trouble with your birth child. Some of you might find a new place for these children to live. That might still be your decision. Up until now you've not been given any alternatives, definitely no support and you have been left on your own to sink or swim. This is not a subject people even want to talk about out loud. It's one to be whispered about, kept quiet and only talked about in hushed tones to a select few. It's too embarrassing to say you've got a two, three, four, up to who knows what age-old child out of control. How can you face people knowing that a small four-year old child is making your life unbearable? Who would want to face that? I see some of the looks on your faces, even some smirks and smiles. Yes, we need to laugh but let's face it, anyone who has lived with an RAD child of any age knows this is no laughing matter for anyone involved. Some of your children also have ODD and ADHD and whatever other acronyms have been added by as many therapists as you've seen. But there is a basic philosophy within these children, some common thread to be addressed after which the main behavior is more agreeable to all involved and life is considerably easier to cope with. Then some of the lesser, yet still important problems can be considered.

What is RAD (Reactive Attachment Disorder) and how in the world can anyone live with it? Let's look at some symptoms:

1. anger that turns into rage
2. anger, destructiveness, cruelty to animals
3. not letting parents close, rejecting them first
4. gratification of needs (food hoarding, head banging)
5. indiscriminately affectionate with strangers
6. won't make eye contact
7. lacks cause and effect thinking
8. poor peer relationships (no friends)
9. fascinated with blood and gore (killing pets, sometimes humans in severe cases)

10. superficially charming
11. disrespect of authority figures
12. self-protects by keeping people at a distance
13. lies, manipulates and steals

Although other children can have some of these symptoms, the important things for us to look at is the fact that this behavior comes from a very different place. For one example, you've got a teenager who hoards food in his room because he gets hungry at night. Teenagers, as we all know, can get lazy, and this one didn't want the bother of running down to the kitchen to get food. He lived with his birth family, who had always loved him and he knew it. He was treated well and knew how to trust and love in return. Now he would have to be disciplined for disobeying the rules BUT would you discipline him the same way as you would discipline another teenager? This second teenager did the exact same thing but his reasons were entirely different. He had been malnourished most of his early life and when he asked for more food he had been smacked around and abused? He didn't trust or love and he was used to sneaking food and saving it so he could be sure to have something to eat later. No, I'm sure you'd agree, the punishment would be different.

What about the very little ones? You know sometimes it's so amazing to me that people ask me a question like this. I adopted my child at two months old. They can't have any memories and so why are they acting so bad at two, three four? That is a very good question and I would like to take a sidebar right now and address it. A mother has carried this child for nine months. It used to be believed that this child had no memories if it was adopted immediately after birth. Now psychologists and professionals have changed their minds and realize that these children couldn't help but have memories. Being within a womb for nine months, you know how your mommy smells, you know the sound of her voice, if she's happy or sad. And listen to this one. The professionals now believe that this child even knows if it was a wanted or unwanted pregnancy. Isn't that amazing? Oh, the human soul. What a complex machine we are. I'm not saying or intimating that they know these things consciously. Of course not. But they know. They really know.

Anyway, back to the little ones. I had a rather interesting experience a few months ago myself. I was in Targets' store looking for a birthday card when all of a sudden a little girl, maybe two or three years old, runs up my aisle and stops right by my side. Looking down at her I notice she's all smiles and says, "What's your name?" to which I reply, "Where's your mom?" She's swaying her little body back and forth and says, "I don't know," without any concern on her face at all. Bells went off immediately in my head. This child is either adopted, a foster child or on the verge RAD for some reason. Why? Think about it. How do little children this age usually act? I've seen many times a little kid this age lose sight of their mommy in a store and start crying immediately. You ask them what's wrong and they say, "Mommy. I can't find my mommy." And that's normal. Listen people, children that age are just like little baby ducks. You know. The mom moves and they follow right behind her and won't lose sight of her. Back to my little friend. Before I had more time to reassess the situation, around the corner comes a frantic mother looking for her little girl. She stops and we talk for a moment and I casually make an inference to which she replies, "Yes, my daughter was adopted just about a year ago," which I already suspected. That child wasn't attached to her yet. The tone of the child's voice when she said, "I don't know where my mommy is," was the definite hint of "I don't care. I don't care if she finds me or not." But that is the difference between little ones attaching and not attaching.

Let's look at some of the causes of RAD and that should give us a clearer picture. What are some of the situations in life that can cause this disorder?

1. unwanted pregnancy
2. neglect
3. inconsistent or inadequate day care
4. dramatic prenatal experience (exposure to drugs/alcohol)
5. sudden separation from the primary caretaker (illness or death)
6. abuse (physical, emotional, mental, sexual)
7. adoption
8. frequent moves (foster care, failed adoptions)

Of course the list goes on and on but these are some of the main reasons. And with that, let's take a break and have some coffee and give yourself time to discuss some of these ideas with people around you. I guarantee that everyone here has been having some similar experiences."

Cindy and Clar met people, talked and just listened to those around them. "My boy killed our family cat last week. I saw him out there playing with it and then he came in and asked for a bowl and some milk. I thought that was good. He apparently put the bowl of milk right in the middle of the sidewalk so he would have better aim when he ran over him with his bike. It just happened so fast I couldn't stop it. And we thought he loved the cat." That was only one story. His boy was presently four years old and adopted at four months old.

Another woman woke up with a butcher knife laid on her chest. That was all. No note. Nothing. But the family was horrified. "My daughter gets very violent. She's almost seven. I have to have one of my older kids sit in the back seat with her to make sure she keeps her seat belt on. Two months ago she tried to choke me while I was driving."

Most parents had tears in their eyes telling stories that seemed like something out of a horror movie. One couple talked for a quite while with the Halls. Their daughter was their birth child and had uncontrollable rages that sounded like Lindsey's. They shared their story of a child who had childhood leukemia and had many lengthy hospital stays about the age of two and was never the same when she returned. Her delightful and fun-loving attitude was gone and never came back. At seven she lied so much and so well that her parents never knew when she was telling the truth or not. Another had a boy who showed strong signs of being abusive but only to his mother and his sister.

Another little girl engaged in crazy lying. She just lied about everything all the time. Lying without a reason was hard to understand.

The stories went on and on. Anger, hate, total rage, uncontrollable hate and destructiveness. Most of the children had some of the symptoms, none had all of them, yet the more symptoms they had, the more serious RAD they were considered. A basic pattern of information was swirling around the room as this was the first time most had heard some of the terminology and definitions being put to some of the behavior exhibited by their children. Now that a definition had been put to some of the behavior, people were anxious to see what, if anything, could be done. As one parent put it, "Now we know what to call it, what do we do about it?" What indeed could you possibly do with this very varied behavior? Then the speaker came back.

"Welcome back. I'm sure you've been given much information from each other to think about. Hopefully your conversations have made you aware of how many different problems are out there. There are literally tons of different behavior possibilities and none very appropriate. And your first questions will probably be how can we possibly deal with such difficult and very different behaviors?

The first thing we have to realize about RAD, of course, is that it can be in different gradations. Some children are only slightly RAD which by the way is an umbrella term for all these problem behaviors and some will be more serious while yet others can be very severe. It does depend on experiences, personalities, neglect, etc. So what are you as parents to do? What can you possibly do?

The first thing to do is to take a deep breath and relax, just relax. That's something you probably haven't done in a long time. You must first take care of yourself because even after your training, you will need a lot of energy. You will find out that it wasn't your fault and that you didn't screw up. You will know that you're not a rotten parent and you will see that other seemingly good successful parents were not dealing with RAD. Take that idea with a long deep breath and know that you really have been as good parent as anyone could be. Now it's time to give yourself a break. You're all working on the last part of your battery and you need to get recharged. So first, take care of yourself. And what do you do with your charming little darlings during that time when you need to relax? You take them to a family member, or a friend, or if none are available, we have respite homes set up for these purposes, but you need to take time out for yourselves and you need to do it every week.

How does going out to dinner just the two of

your sound? Or if you are single, how about joining friends for an evening out without worry? You've got to do it. You have to take time and show the children that you think enough of yourself to go out and have fun. That's good role modeling. So first, take care of yourself.

Then you have to find a qualified RAD therapist, not just a good therapist but a good qualified RAD therapist. Why is that? Because they have the special training and they know the techniques to use with RAD children. Ordinary therapy usually won't work. Let me give you an example. What does ordinary therapy consist of? Usually a good therapist will take the time during the first few visits to build up a relationship, a trust with the child and when they have done this, they will move on to their problems. But RAD children do **not** trust; they have relationship problems. They have been taught not to trust by adults who were supposed to tend to their needs, love them and nurture them but instead their needs were not met; they were ignored and instead of love they were abused, physically, mentally, emotionally and/or sexually. This cannot be overcome by a few sessions of just talking. And to be honest, talking only, doesn't seem to get to the children. Usually RAD therapists will treat these children by enabling them to experience, feel and do that which will help them to internalize new ways of thinking toward life. It's not an easy or quick process. There's not much progress at first, so you have to hang in there and be happy with small positive results. These children have been hurt very, very deeply and at an age where they could not yet analyze selectively for themselves that the entire world is not hurtful in this way.

Many RAD children really believe that love is supposed to be painful. Not a fun way to live, is it?

And you were all wondering why they didn't respond when you showed them love and kindness. Most were taught at an early age by experiencing neglect. They cried for hours and no one came. When they tried to show love to an alcoholic mother, they were smacked or even beat up and yet, they knew this was the same woman who also said she loved them at other times. Mom loves me and she constantly hurts me so love must be painful. Let's say the child is a girl and now as she grows up, she's looking for male companionship. She finds someone who tells her over and over again that he loves her, but he smacks her around and generally treats her very badly. She reminds herself that this is what my mother did so this must be love. And the cycle continues.

Can you see how complex our thinking can be? We humans perceive and accept experiences as truth until someone comes along to show us a different way. This same little girl is in elementary school. Do you think she would have a strong capacity to trust adults and want to obey the rules? It's a vicious cycle. Add this to the fact that she knows her mother gave her away. Was I a bad kid? Why did she give me away? Moms aren't supposed to give their kids away. This little girl would be one example of a child whose early experiences color how she looks at everything in the world. Would she see the world in the same way as a child born and staying in a loving family where her security, love and a nurturing atmosphere is not constantly questioned. Of course not. This second child has the ideal chance of becoming a well-adjusted and self-confident adult barring any significant unforeseen negative experiences.

Therein lies some of the differences between birth children and adopted children. All birth children do not have the perfect scenarios in their lives, but for our discussion we compare with those that do. Just for the record, no one has a perfect childhood either. Anyway, this is just a basic overview of why these children act as they do. I wanted you to have an idea of what they deal with internally. It's a rough road for these kids but just as tough for you parents especially before you have any understanding of their internal reasoning for their behavior."

Clar and Cindy left the lecture wide-eyed but excited at what they had heard.

"Imagine all the times that we tried to tell her how much we loved her," said Cindy feeling frustrated, "remember, how she used to just look at us."

"Yeah, she couldn't really believe it. Maybe we should have given her love in little doses?"

"Or showed her that we loved her. Words are easy to say, but actions count too."

"Now that I understand a little more, I can see why she couldn't believe us, even if she wanted to."

"She always kept her distance," continued Clar. "We'd try to pull her into the close circle with us, but she never totally relaxed, you know. But looking at life from her point of view, how could she?"

"I remember once, in the early days, when I sent her to her room for something. I heard her say, 'I knew this wouldn't last.' I didn't pay that much attention at the time, but now... I think she thought of it as a total rejection of her person, rather than just being disciplined for one action. Big difference."

Clar added. "I'm sure that Irene would think of it as one

episode and not take it that personally."

"This is an entire education, you know. She thinks very differently than we do and I can see that now. If only we had known."

"But Cindy, we didn't know. That must be what April wanted us to realize. Then you and I and her can all be on the same page and treat her exactly the same way. That would give her a solid base. I think we wasted time but we didn't know."

"We should have found time to take these classes before but ..."

"Life has given us all a second chance," Clar added, "and this time we'll get it right. I mean, just listen to us talk now. We are trying to figure out the best way to handle things, we are devising a philosophy and whatever. Before we just gave up and were ready to take her back. You were ready to collapse and so was I. But look, we have hope and there is a way."

"Doesn't mean it will be easy, but there's a way and that makes a big difference. We can work with April and it's like being part of a team. And that's what these kids need. Teacher, parents, babysitters, aunts and uncles, everyone all working with the same philosophy." Cindy saw Clar nod in agreement. She too had enthusiasm – and that made a lot of difference.

One man had asked the question if there was an age when it was too late to help these children. The encouraging reply was that they could always be helped, although the older the child the longer and possibly more in depth the therapy would be, but all could be helped.

The last comment was a good final point. Would these children ever be normal? The answer was as normal as any child can be. No child is perfect so that wasn't the goal. Yet if they could go from being hateful, rage-filled, totally rebellious, unloving and untrusting, angry children and become thoughtful and respectful, nice to be around, then this would be considered success. And with the right tools and the right team all working together, it would succeed.

# Chapter Four

Within the next few months, major changes were seen again in Lindsey's behavior. She had turned twelve now and with adolescence zooming in, April wanted Lindsey's feet back on solid ground. April's sessions were more intense.

April said, "You've turned twelve years old now and you're getting to a new phase in your life. How do you feel about it?"

Lindsey said, "I think about it a lot. It's kind of confusing to me. I'm about to get to a point where I have to start thinking about a future, not right away but soon, which to me means I've got to decide where I want to go with my life and I'm not sure where I've been. Know what I mean?"

April nodded as she watched Lindsey's changing expressions trying to figure out her philosophy. Lindsey's attitude was much better in the last few months as she had again regained some stability in her life.

"You know, a lot of kids don't have to think about the things on my mind," Lindsey continued. "I mean, lately I feel better about my parents, but they're not my birth parents. That's still something I have to think about. How can I know who I am and what I want to become when I'm not real sure where I've been? Sounds funny when I put it into words, but it's often on my mind. Who am I really?"

"How do you feel when you think about it? Are you comfortable, mad, relaxed, angry or what?"

"I'm not angry like I used to be, but it still bothers me. It does depress me a little and I think, 'gees, Lindsey you've known this all your life so when is it going to stop bothering you.' And I want to ask you, Ms. April. When is it going to stop bothering me? Will it ever stop?"

April saw Lindsey look down at the floor and try to figure out her feelings. She was a very thoughtful child, at the moment slightly angry and confused as her slight pout brought to mind the younger child she remembered.

"I'm not sure how you'll think about it when you're older. But tell me Lindsey, does it bother you as much and in the same way as when I first met you? At six years old you were very, very angry, I'm sure you remember. I don't think you get as angry now. Do you?"

"No, but it still bothers me."

"But that's okay. Adults have a lot of things 'bother them,' as you say. That's when we have to figure out a solution logically."

"But I'm not an adult. I'm not even a teenager yet."

"That's very true Lindsey. But, you've also grown from being a very frightened six year old who went into rages and now, even though you still get mad and hurt, you're in control. That's better isn't it?"

"It would be strange if I went into rages now."

"Many adults haven't conquered their fears and still need help. Some adults go into rages just like you did when you were little. But you know what? Their consequences are much worse for them because they are older and when they are over eighteen or twenty-one and break the law, they can go to jail and can be in a lot of trouble."

"But I don't do that anymore. I've finally got that under control, mostly. And I still miss that class you know."

"Yeah, we did have a great year, didn't we? I'm proud that you don't have rages anymore that's a lot of progress for you. But you did have problems obeying the rules and listening to your teachers. Also, you got into a few fights in class."

"I still can get mad at times, but I don't go into rages. I hated that feeling it was awful. I do better now, don't you think? I do better now that you're back here."

"What do **you** think?"

"My math teacher told me the other day that she's pleased with my behavior. And last week my history teacher told me that she liked how much I've changed and hoped that I continue. The other teachers haven't said anything yet, and they watch me a lot, but I haven't gotten into much trouble."

"Why do you think that is?"

"Because you're back. I've told you."

"Me being back didn't magically make everything all right. Why do you think things are better now?"

April saw Lindsey staring into space for a few minutes. Slowly she came back to reality and began trying to explain what happened to her.

"I'd like to tell you but I'm not sure I can put it into words. But it's sort of because I know you understand, know what I mean? We've talked about it. I know that you don't totally know how I feel but it helps so much when someone around me knows that I don't think and feel like some of the others around me. I have learned that everyone thinks differently because we've all had different experiences in our lives. That makes sense to me. And when I talk to some of the kids in my classes I know that they think in a lot of ways that don't agree with each other. The teacher says that's what makes us individuals."

"You've got a good handle on that approach?"

"But, they think differently, yet their beginnings were the same. There are only a few other adoptees in this school that I know of. Maybe we would think more alike, but I don't really know them. It's like the other day I was talking to this girl and she said that her mom didn't want her to do something and she fought with her but the girl finally won. She wasn't fighting and thinking, 'I'd better not go beyond a certain point because they could send me back where I came from.' Maybe that sounds silly, but even now, I think they might want to send me away. Don't tell them, okay?"

"I don't tell your parents anything we talk about. This is private between us. But what you just said is a fact of your life. You were adopted and you can't change that. But you're twelve years old, now, so I think maybe they'll keep you, right?"

"Oh I know that when I think it out. It's when I get my feelings all twisted inside that I worry about it."

"Worry isn't always bad. It just keeps you aware."

"You know, I still think about my birth mom and dad and wonder who they are and what they're like. I just can't help but wonder sometimes."

"That's okay Lindsey. That's normal."

"But I still don't talk to my mom and dad. And I never mention it to Irene, you know."

"Maybe they'd be okay with it now. What do you think?"

"I don't know, but now that everything's going better I'd rather leave it alone and not upset the household. It just seems that as long as I can mention her to you sometimes, then she seems real to me. And I need that."

"Okay Lindsey, and you can do that anytime."

For Clar and Cindy it was the best and most wondrous thing to learn that they didn't have to be angry all the time. Lindsey really wanted their anger. She dealt with anger much better than she dealt with love and kindness, because inside she was still in a lot of turmoil. But that's not what she needed. Lindsey, first of all needed laughter, lots of laughter. Kids filled with rage really don't laugh much because they are so sad inside. So they need laughter. Then they need empathy, understanding without anger. And always they need unconditional love. Clar and Cindy always reminded each other of these facts.

"I've started writing out these little cards with the rules we've just learned. I wrote them out so that when I'm in a turmoil and can't think straight, I just pull out one of my cards to remind myself what I need to do for her benefit and for mine as well."

"Good idea. Let me see that."

Cindy said, "What do you think? Helps me, when I just can't think."

"We should spread this around. It's a good idea."

"Oh Clar, I didn't think of it. Remember at last month's

meeting I was talking to that trainer for a while, she mentioned this and I love the idea. I'm someone who sometimes just freezes during turmoil. And this really helps me."

"We're due for a weekend away by ourselves and I'm so looking forward to it. I've talked to our group and found out about a few respite workers. I figure your sister can take care of Irene for two nights. She never minds. But now I know that Lindsey will be safe and with someone who knows about her."

"I think Lindsey couldn't believe it the first time we went away," said Clar. Then he added sarcastically. "Or maybe she couldn't believe we returned."

Weekends away restored their sense of humor and helped them to gain the strength they needed to work with Lindsey. Although her behavior was better and she was improving quite satisfactorily, they always had to be prepared with her and to act within their boundaries. If Lindsey even thought she might get the upper hand, she would have a setback and then all suffered.

One example was skating on Friday night. Lindsey loved to roller skate at the local arena since most of the students were from her school and she had a chance to socialize without ever having to have close friends. She very seldom ever went with friends since her peer relationships were always in trouble, yet she wanted to be there. Coming alone enabled her to have fun without getting too close to anyone. For Lindsey, this worked out very well.

It was important for Lindsey to get to the roller arena at a certain time. Kids stood in line together and wanted to be the first to enter. So every Friday night at 6:00 PM Lindsey expected someone to drive her to the arena. Many times Lindsey's chores were not done, which was a constant battle.

There were always arguments and tempers raging because she just wouldn't cooperate. But now Clar and Cindy had learned that they didn't have to get angry and argue with Lindsey. So when she came out of her room Friday at precisely 6:00 PM, expecting someone to drop what they were doing to drive her roller-skating, she was in for a different parenting system.

"Mom, it's 6:00 PM. Let's go. I have to get to the roller rink."

Cindy noted that Lindsey had left a total mess of clothes, makeup, hair equipment and scrap paper all over the family room. This was always the argument and 'I'll do it later' was always the comment thrown out with the expectation that someone else would do it sooner before her later came.

"Come on mom, let's go," Lindsey repeated.

"Can you see the car in the driveway, Lindsey? It's all ready to go and I'll drive you to roller skating just as soon as the family room is cleaned up."

That being said, Cindy proceeded to walk to the stove to make herself a cup of tea, leaving Lindsey with her mouth open, roller skates in her hands and a very shocked look on her face.

"Come on, Mom, you're kidding right? Come on, we have to go now or I'll be late."

Cindy never broke a sweat and kept a very nice and caring tone in her voice as she said, "I know, Lindsey, and I'll drive you as soon as my family room is cleaned up of your stuff."

"For God's sakes, mom, this is really crappy. I'll do it tomorrow."

Although she was tempted, Cindy decided not to tell Lindsey that she would therefore drive her to roller skating tomorrow. She didn't even answer at all, having made her cup of tea, she headed for her room.

"Mom, damn it, where are you going? We've go to leave." She could see that Lindsey was quite angry, but in control, and she was not about to give up.

Cindy, being very careful not to show anger, simply answered, "I'm going to my room to watch TV for a while, but you let me know as soon as our family room is cleaned up and I'll drive you to the rink."

With that Cindy went to her room and closed the door, leaving Lindsey in disbelief. Immediately Cindy heard a flurry of activity and within fifteen minutes there was a light tap on her door followed by a very nicely toned request. "Mom, can you come and see if the family room is okay?"

"Why, this looks just fine. Get your stuff together and we can leave right now."

This was the first time that Cindy had gotten Lindsey to do chores without having anger on both sides, intermittent screaming and hollering, and occasional frightening behavior. Life was slowly changing in the Hall household and Lindsey was changing with it.

Amusement found its way back into the Halls' home and many times Irene and Lindsey could hear their parents laughing out loud and having fun together. Lindsey's anger considerably lessened since no one reacted, except possibly Irene. They still didn't blend very well so Clar and Cindy used the same philosophy on Irene and it helped her too.

With continued therapy, the sessions with Ms. April sometimes took on new conversation.

"My parents really act different now," Lindsey said in a rather guarded tone.

"What do you mean different, is that good or bad?"

"Sometimes, it's just weird. They laugh a lot now. Honestly it really used to irritate me, but now I don't mind it too much. I don't know what they find to laugh about all the time."

"So you like the change in them."

"Not sure if I really like it, but I don't mind it much. Irene thinks it's weird too."

"Does Irene like it or not?"

"Not sure. We don't always talk a lot. But we've talked about our parents. I mean I know before I was more trouble to them and they argued and mom cried a lot. But now she's always laughing. And even when I don't always do what I should do, she doesn't get mad or upset."

"What does she do?"

"It's hard to say. The other day she just made a cup of tea and went into her room to watch TV by herself for a while. I wanted to get my homework done so I wouldn't put away the dishes. She didn't even argue with me. She just went into her room."

"Okay, maybe she just needed to be by herself for a while. You know how you like that."

"But she didn't put the dishes away. After I finished my homework and was ready to go to bed, I had to put the dishes away. And I was tired and had to go to school the next day. But she still made me do it."

"Did you think that wasn't fair?"

"She was right, I know. But she didn't get mad. She's acting really strange lately. And dad's the same way. They stick together all the time now. That makes it tough."

"What does it make tough?"

Suddenly Lindsey looked suspiciously at Ms. April and seemed to realize the game she was playing. "You know, don't you? It makes it tough to get my own way anymore. I have to follow the rules. If I don't, nobody gets mad anymore and nobody yells and screams and there usually aren't any of those lectures I hated. I just don't do it. But then the job doesn't get done. So if we don't have any dishes the next day, guess who has to hurry up and get them ready for dinner? I do." Even Lindsey had to laugh about the routine that was set up.

"Seems to me that's what makes the household run smoothly, when everyone does his job, right?"

Lindsey gave Ms. April a very noncommittal look and decided she wasn't winning this battle either. Grown ups were all acting strange now. The only good thing was that she knew what to expect from them.

As Lindsey graduated from middle school and moved on to high school, her parents had learned from their first mistake and wanted April to remain a mentor in Lindsey's life. So, they still met, not as often, and not always in a formal setting. It was emails and phone contacts and some lunches. And although her problems were not totally behind her, they were now under control and she was getting solid help on all sides from a very powerful team.

Time moved on quickly and Lindsey went to college working on a degree in Accounting. But today, they were meeting for dinner and as she entered the Horizon restaurant,

Ms. April stood up and motioned her over. Lindsey was usually the second person to arrive, but she was never very late. They hugged and laughed and always talked about those days in special first grade as well as middle school.

"You know, Ms. April, I did some investigating on my own. It was all hush-hush, but I found the adoption agency where they got me. I contacted them and asked them if they knew the lady who handled my case. At first, they were hesitant but told me to call back in a few days." Lindsey watched April's expression as she began telling her one of the secrets of her life. As usual, her expression was blank.

"That was a big step for you," April commented.

"But it was something I needed to do. Anyway, when I called back they told me that nothing was signed about a closed adoption so they saw no harm in discussing my adoption, but cautioned there wasn't much information anyway. I made an appointment with a Ms. Niles, who wasn't the original caseworker, but willing to talk to me."

"That was risky, wasn't it? I assume you didn't tell your parents."

"No, I never could talk to them. And that was one of the conditions that I told the adoption agency. I wasn't looking to try and find her. I just wanted to know something, anything at all about my birth mother or birth father. Ms Niles didn't know very much but guess what she did? She had talked to a Mrs. Lacey, who is retired now but she was the original caseworker and she agreed to meet me for lunch."

"Wow, when did this take place?"

"About two months ago, after I turned twenty-one so she didn't see any harm. Actually she always believed that us adoptees should be given the information. She really was a rebel-type caseworker, I understand."

"That's good," April said laughing, "I'd have to agree with her on that."

"Anyway, she remembered very little it was a long time ago. But she did remember my mother. You know why? She was very nervous and when she came in with me, she talked to Mrs. Lacey for a long time. And Mrs. Lacey was new to the job and she was nervous too. I understand she came in twice before she made the decision. That was good to know. She didn't just dump me the first time anyway."

"Are you all right with this information; this had to be quite difficult?"

"Not knowing anything was harder. And you know, Ms. April, you and I had talked so much about her. That was the great part. You let me dream and tell stories about what I thought she might be like and what had really happened to her which forced her to abandon me. I think I must have dreamt up every possible story so that now, when I heard just a little part of it, it was okay. Remember too, I'm older and stronger now. I've studied psychology in college and I'm learning all the time, just like you said."

"Lindsey, you impress me more all the time. So what else did Mrs. Lacey tell you?"

"She said that the first time my mom came in she was upset about giving me up. She seemed young, not more than twenty. And she wasn't married. You know she told the story that her husband left and didn't want the baby. And, he didn't want the baby that was true, but they didn't get married. On one paper she said they got married, and put down a marriage date, but she changed the date the next time she was in. And when asked about the discrepancy, she cried and admitted they never got married. She was pregnant at seventeen and her parents were furious and wouldn't help her. She actually left home because she didn't want to give up her baby. You see, she really wanted to keep me." Lindsey paused for a moment as her voice quivered. "She told Mrs. Lacey that her so-called husband at first wanted to get married but then he got tired of a baby quickly when he found out how expensive it was. After he left, she tried for a little while but couldn't care for me all alone. Mrs. Lacey told me that day when the record sheet said that she left because she was mad, it wasn't true. Mrs. Lacey remembers, 'cause that was one of her first cases ever and said that my mother was crying hard and couldn't control herself. Everyone did think that she would come back later, but she didn't. Maybe she couldn't."

"Quite a story. Makes you feel sorry for your mom too, doesn't it? Some girls get into these impossible situations. It's too bad. How does all this information make you feel?"

"I'm real sad about everything but at least it wasn't that she didn't want me. I'm sure I could never contact her because Mrs. Lacey said that it wasn't her real name on the record file. And that's not unusual. I'm not sure how I would search if I wanted to."

"Do you want to do that?"

"No, I don't think so. I wouldn't upset my parents that way. I don't even want them to find out what I did, but if it ever came up, I wouldn't lie about it. They might be okay with it now, but why take the chance on hurting them? I found out what I wanted to know and it helped a lot. I can pray for her at night now and wish her a good life. I think she must have had a rough time. I hope she ended up happy."

"You're so grown up now. How very mature you are."

"It's about time. I've become who I am because of my

parents and because of you. And I like who I am. I'm okay with me so I can afford to have sympathy. You taught me that a long time ago in those little reading circles, remember? That is when I learned to sit in someone else's place and see how it would feel to be them. I never forgot that."

Then Ms. April tossed out a tough question for Lindsey. "If you could, what would you change about your life?"

"What do you mean? Would I wish I were never adopted and had good birth parents? Of course I do. That would have been the best. But you know, I do believe that my birth mother would have been a good mother, if she'd had the chance."

"Yes, of course, but that didn't happen. So being you were adopted, what would you change?"

"I wouldn't change my parents and they really are my parents. I wouldn't change them like I thought I wanted to do. I probably wouldn't even change Irene, although we only learned to tolerate each other we never really liked each other. I think we did learn to understand each other, or rather I learned to understand Irene. I know she never understood me."

"Do you love your family Lindsey?"

"Yes I do, I really do. I love mom and dad and I even love Irene, although I don't much like her sometimes. But I do love her – we're family. Our relationship is just different."

Sitting comfortably mulling over a glass of wine after a good meal, was a perfect setting for conversation. Lindsey no longer recoiled at the thought of probing questions. She was used to Ms. April and still felt she was the only one who truly understood her.

"But what would you change Lindsey? You haven't answered me."

"First, I don't want to change any people but I wish mom and dad had understood more what was going on inside of me, especially when I was very young. I admire them a lot for contacting you the second time. They really tried to understand me by going to all those lectures and seminars and classes and our home became happier and we had lots of fun times."

"They're good people and they really love you."

"I know and I wasn't easy to love for a very long time."

"They understood your pain later and they admired you for your strength and determination."

"They put so much effort into helping me and they know now how much I appreciate them as parents. That's what a real mom and dad do, just what they did. They're there for you when you need them. I was lucky to get them."

"Okay, but what would you change?"

"Oh yeah, what would I change? I'm thinking of how to say it because I don't know if this could be changed because I know that mom and dad tried but ..."

"Yes, but what? Just say it."

"Okay, here it is. I would never have a chance to find my dad; he was just gone, and actually my mom was gone too. But I wished my adoptive parents could have known why I had such a need to talk about my birth mom, especially. They just got so mad and angry when I mentioned her. I was so little then but I knew she gave me life. Whatever else she did or didn't do or couldn't do, she did give me life and she's my beginning and this mom and dad are my end. Do you know what I mean?"

"Pretty deep Lindsey. Yes, she'll always be your birth mother."

"Yes, and I'll always think about that. That'll never go away. I didn't expect them to know how I felt, even you couldn't know that, it's just that sometimes I had such a need to mention her. It kept her alive in my mind and if I lost that, then I lost part of myself."

"I see. And now?"

"I don't need to talk about her much anymore, at least not out loud. Now that I know something about her, it helps. Sometimes though I still try to remember how she looked and how she smelled but I really can't, but I still try. When I try real hard, I can almost remember her laughter. I see the look on your face. Yes, maybe I'm just pretending, but I still need to do that. But it doesn't hurt much anymore. Yet, it's still there you know, the need to make her real once in a while."

"You're right that I could never know how you feel about that."

"But you always empathized with me, Ms. April and that was all I needed at the time. Someone who would confirm to me that it had really happened and it was okay to have those feelings. You helped me with the hurt those feelings caused. My parents wouldn't let me talk about her out loud, yet that didn't make the feelings and the hurt go away. They didn't make her disappear from my mind and memory just because they wouldn't let me mention her."

"I think you've earned the right to call me April."

Lindsey laughed. "To me, you'll always be Ms. April. You know why? It's part of the kid in me. You were the first one to validate my feelings and in my mind I probably will always think of us as we were back in that special class."

"We're both older now but if that's what you want, you can call me Ms. April."

"You will always be Ms. April to me," Lindsey said very affectionately.

"So you would have changed being able to talk about your birth mother, at least once in a while?"

"I would have liked them to let me talk about her, the only one of my parents I truly remembered and sometimes I even needed to mention my dad, but I don't remember him at all. But these parents always hated it when I mentioned them; you could see them cringe and the atmosphere in the room really changed. And then there was Irene always telling me that I should just appreciate what I had. And I did appreciate it. But Irene had her birth mom and dad, right there in the same house and didn't know what it felt like to be given away. Look at me now, I'm an adult woman of twenty-one, and if I talk too much about being given away, I could still cry. I live fine with it all but it never really goes away."

"Yes, Lindsey, that feeling runs deep and I know it would always be there for me too."

"All I needed was to be able to talk about her sometimes, but I couldn't. Maybe they felt I didn't love them if I talked about her, but the two things had nothing to do with each other. Yet that's what they made me feel."

"That would have been tough."

"However, I don't blame them anymore. I did for a long time, you know, and maybe that's why it took me so long to trust them. No one's perfect. They did so many things right except they couldn't handle the baggage I came with. But I could always talk to you and that helped. That was such a deep need for me though and that's why I think I'll always have a special bond with you. I love you, you know.

"Oh sweetie, I have always loved you."

"All in all they're great parents and I wouldn't trade them. Considering how my life turned out, they adopted and then I met you, who really started my life, I think I've been kind of lucky anyway."

"I'm glad you feel that way. I feel blessed to have known you."

"Yeah, I love my parents and even Irene but everyone needs someone who really understands and I've got you."

"I guess that says it all."

"Yes it does, and Life is Good." Lindsey's voice trailed off and they both sat there in their own thoughts, smiling over a glass of wine.

# SECTION II

# THE STORY OF EDDIE SABERS

# Chapter One

Eddie Sabers couldn't believe how huge the headlines were as he grabbed the newspaper that had been placed next to him on the small table in his holding cell. "THREE BOYS ARRESTED ON DRUG BUST. He just stared at the last two words, "DRUG BUST." The way the newspaper was set up, it forced you to see only the headlines and they just glared at you, shocking your senses with their skillful presentation. He had really done it this time. The downward spiral of his life was quickly reaching the bottom rung on the ladder and Eddie wished he knew how his life had gotten so out of control.

"Eddie Sabers?" One of the guards called his name.

"Yes, I'm Eddie Sabers," he answered.

"Did you get dinner yet today?" asked the guard.

"I didn't get anything to eat," he replied in a firm tone, not really polite but not rude either. He regretted already having spent two days in jail.

"You didn't get lunch at 12:00?" the guard asked, stopping right in front of the door of his cell.

"No, I didn't."

"Gees, heh Willy, here's another one that was missed.

We'll bring you something soon," he yelled as he walked on to the next cell.

The last few years had been just one nightmare after another stealing hubcaps, mostly for quick money, lying to everyone about everything, getting suspended from Hawthorne High for fighting, and finally expelled. Eddie thought, *What has happened to me? I showed promise at one time at basketball and my grades were good. BUT look at Eddie Sabers now, and I'm only sixteen years old.*

After finally eating lunch, Eddie sat around thinking. *There isn't anything else to do except to sit around and I don't want to look at the newspaper again. I feel like crying, except that I can't cry, I'm supposed to be a man.. Imagine at my age and I still feel like crying sometimes.*

"Eddie Sabers, up to the door," called the guard. "Yes," he answered feeling very unsure of himself.

"It'll be your turn to go before the judge in ten minutes. Be ready. Do you have any questions before you go?"

"No, I guess not," he answered, lacking any clear thought on his mind.

"Do you have anyone here to represent you?" The guard had a check sheet which he kept writing on during their conversation.

"No, I don't know anybody," Eddie admitted reluctantly.

"You were allowed to make a phone call," said the guard reminding him of his legal rights.

"I didn't know anyone to call." Eddie had spent the last two nights trying to think of someone who might help him. No name came to his mind.

"Gees," was all the guard said. "Good luck."

Ten minutes passed and the guard came back. "Let's go Eddie; it's your turn." It was time to go before the judge and he knew this was the beginning of the end for him. There was no one there for him. His so-called friends, Joe and Timmy had influential families who had posted bail two days ago. This drug job was Tim's idea and he had done all the persuasion. But it had gone wrong, really, really wrong. Eddie had no one to blame but himself and he knew it. He had made the decision to go along just for quick money.

As he looked around the courtroom from his isolated bench, he felt old thoughts of loneliness return. He was here alone, as he had been always alone, since he was four years old. Only once did he ever believe he belonged in this world, and that was in one foster home. Then, for the first time he had really known the feeling of belonging. That was a while ago and too painful to remember. As he waited, Eddie thought back on his early life through the very cloudy images that he could remember. Some he remembered consciously and others he had been told about. Did he actually remember being in that playground almost twelve years ago or had someone just told him about it? He didn't know any more.

"Heh little boy, are you here all alone?" A smiling lady was standing next to him as he sat on the swings.

Eddie looked up wondering if he should answer. He decided not to answer.

"What's your name?" she asked, trying again to talk to him.

"Eddie." he answered.

"Well, Eddie, where's your mom?"

Eddie just shrugged his shoulders as he looked around. The lady was still smiling at him and soon she was joined by another lady.

"I think he's here alone. I don't see anyone around. Let's wait five minutes and then we should call someone, don't you think?"

"Yes," said the other lady, "I think so. He's clean, recent haircut. I'll bet someone is starting to panic about him. Maybe we should just take him to the police station."

"Do you know where your mommy is?"

Eddie never answered but he started crying. After five minutes passed and no parents or babysitter came looking for Eddie, the ladies took him to the police station. His rescuers didn't know much, just that he was alone at the playground, with no adult around and they felt it was too dangerous to leave him there alone.

At the police station were more questions. "What's your name?" asked one police officer.

"Eddie, my name is Eddie." "Okay, Eddie, what's your last name?" The officer couldn't understand his last name so he called over a friend who also found the name undetectable. Even after he had repeated it a few times, no one was sure what he was saying. It sounded like Saberson or Sabersden or Saberton, but that was only a guess. So, on his file was entered the name Sabers, the only part of his name that people could understand.

"How old are you Eddie?" Another question.

"I'm four," he answered. He didn't remember his phone number or his address.

"Where's your mom," he was asked.

"I don't know," Eddie said as the officer watched him as he shrugged his shoulders and looked down at the floor while he rocked his body from side to side. He answered again that he didn't know where his mommy was. He appeared very frightened and was fighting back tears.

"Who took you to the playground?" Yet another question from another officer.

"My mommy," said Eddie in a voice that trembled and stuttered slightly, making his speech pattern difficult to understand at times. They noticed his mouth would go into a self-inflicted pout when he was asked more questions than he obviously wanted to answer. Eddie's feet didn't even come close to touching the floor from the chair he was put on and he seemed to just sit there and watch people in the huge room as they came up to him for a moment and then quickly moved away.

"I guess we'll have to start working the phone lines and see what comes up," said the sergeant. "Anything on TV or radio? Any report at all come in about a missing kid. He seems clean enough and well taken care of. Hair cut recently, clean, fairly new clothes. We should hear something soon."

"He sure looks nervous and scared; I guess any kid would," said George Bowers, a policeman who had wandered into the precinct on his day off. Looking at this little kid George felt his fear at not finding anyone he could trust in the room as he kept looking at all of the guns that the officers were wearing. He looked as if he was cowering in his chair.

"Have you ever been to school?" asked George.

Eddie didn't answer and George watched him as looked from one person to another with his eyes blinking often and moving very quickly. Nervousness was overtaking his body and his head went down while his hands started shaking a little. George tried again. "Have you been to kindergarten yet?"

"No," he answered, "I'm four." Then it started. He could see the fear in Eddie's face and could tell it was spreading throughout his body as he began to hunch up in his chair. George tried again to talk soft and nice, hoping to calm him down a little.

"Your mommy took you to the playground right? Was your daddy there too?" he asked.

"Don't have a daddy. Got some uncles sometimes but no daddy," replied Eddie.

"Did you walk to the playground or did you go in a car?" George managed to sit next to him in the very large chair and Eddie didn't move away.

"In a car, big car that's blue like the sky. Smelled funny. I was in the back seat."

"Did you have a seat belt on?" continued George, hoping to keep Eddie talking as more information might come out of his mouth.

"Yes, belt was tight. Mom was crying and yelling. Then the car stopped and mommy took me over to the swings. She pushed me so I could go high. Then gone, and so was the car. I was waiting for her. Will she know where I am?"

"We're trying to find your mommy now," said George trying to reassure him.

Eddie asked again, "Where's my mommy?"

He had to answer, "We don't know right now, but we're trying to find her, okay?"

Then Eddie started to cry and George watched him as he tried to stop the tears from coming down on his cheeks, but he couldn't.

As the clock hit 10:00 PM at the precinct and nobody had called to report a missing child, social services was contacted and Eddie was taken to a short term foster home. The lady was nice and gave him some tomato soup and a sandwich but then as they gave him sleeping clothes he got very agitated.

"This isn't my bedroom. You're not my mommy. Where's my mommy?" he asked.

"We are looking for your mommy but you must be tired so I'm gonna put you to sleep, okay?"

"How will my mommy find me here? Do you know my mommy?"

"No, I don't know your mommy but the police will tell her where you are."

As Eddie was tucked into bed he was very nervous. He'd never seen these people before; they were strangers to him. And Eddie didn't trust strangers. He didn't know where he was. This wasn't his bed. And where was his mommy?

Eddie stayed at this foster home for almost a month. In all that time not one person ever called the police asking about a missing little boy. Eddie kept waiting for his mom, but she never came. He got more and more quiet and much more withdrawn every day. He liked the lady here, she talked nicely to him and gave him cookies, but Eddie wanted his mom.

"When is my mom coming to get me?" he would ask at least ten times a day.

"The police are looking for her but haven't found her yet." That was the standard reply. The lady always said the same thing so Eddie persisted.

"Are they really trying? I told them she had a blue car and she's real tall and has black hair and is very pretty. My mom's very pretty," he said before the tears would come. The adults were trying by now to enter the possibility into his mind that his mom might not come back. But Eddie always got hysterical when the idea was mentioned and it was decided not to mention it anymore until he was a bit older. Days passed as Eddie just sat and looked out the window waiting and waiting for his mom, but she never came. He kept looking for a big blue car, the color of the sky and was worried that his mom might not be able to find this place. The police showed Eddie the posters that were put around the city and Eddie even saw his picture on TV, but still no response. No one seemed to know who Eddie was or if he even came from this city. Finally, a decision had to be made about Eddie.

"Well, Eddie," said the nice lady, "you're going to be moving to another place now."

"No, I can't. I'm waiting for my mommy," he answered stubbornly.

"You can wait for your mom at the other place too. The police will tell her where you are."

"Why can't I stay here?" he asked.

"Because it's time for you to move to the other place." answered the short-term foster mother. Eddie would never understand that she took children in for short-terms only and now he was being moved to a more permanent foster home. And he didn't understand anything she said and started crying.

"But I like you, don't you like me?"

"Yes, I like you. You've been a real good boy. But you'll like the lady at the new place too. She's very nice and they have a bigger back yard there." The lady's voice had a different tone in it. It wasn't mad exactly, but it wasn't as nice anymore.

"Okay," said Eddie and he got very quiet. He didn't say another word. He just waited, too scared even to ask anything about the new place.

"I'm sure you'll like your new home Eddie."

Eddie tried to smile but didn't quite succeed. He just went back to his room and packed his little bag which only had a toothbrush and a pair of pajamas.

"Eddie's not taken this very well. He got used to me," she told the social worker. "What are his chances at the other foster home?"

"Well," said the social worker, "there will still be many attempts to find his parents. The law still remains on the side of the parents. If they're found and don't have any interest in the child or they can't take care of the child, there's still much paperwork needed to terminate their rights so that he could be permanently adopted."

"And we both know everything takes so much time in this system."

"Yes, that's true, and so Eddie will have years of foster homes ahead of him. And if they can't find either parent, it will take quite a while before all avenues are followed and by then he will be much older and have less chance of being adopted at all."

"Here he comes down the stairs with his little bag. This

is such a sad moment for him. He was adjusting quite well to this place. He's been with me a month."

Eddie looked at the two women waiting for him at the bottom of the stairs and thought, *It must be nice to be a big person and be able to go where you wanted to go.* He wondered, *where will they take me now? What will happen to me? Who will take care of me? And where is my mom?*

The second foster home had too many children and Eddie was moved again after only two weeks and put into another temporary foster home. This temporary arrangement lasted for over three years. Again many children came and went and nothing seemed very permanent for Eddie. Adults came and went out of his life too and no one ever stayed for long. This last foster home he never liked. He always felt that he was visiting and never felt that it was his home. There wasn't much supervision and some of the older kids could be mean.

"I don't mind kicking your ass, you little nothing if you don't get out of my way," said Keith. Whenever he threatened anyone, he always had this certain hysterical laugh that sounded like a hyena. Keith enjoyed tormenting and scaring the younger children. He was sixteen himself and life had been nasty to him. He didn't mind passing cruelty on to anyone that would accept it. That was all the younger kids because he wasn't stupid or brave enough to pick on kids his own age.

"Sorry," said Eddie. He had learned not to irritate Keith. Once Keith had punched him in the stomach so hard that he vomited all night.

"Yeah, right, you're sorry. Don't even come near me, cause I'm older and I'm stronger. I've been here longer and I've got all the rights, stupid kid," said Keith as he stomped his feet on the floor. This sent Eddie running away as fast as he could to escape any torture Keith had on his mind. It also sent Keith laughing wildly as this was how he spent his days and nights.

During these years, Eddie learned how to be alone. Shortly after his sixth birthday he began to be a loner and depended mostly on himself because he felt safer that way. There were no adults around who really cared about him and he had no friends. He learned to stay away from Keith and to mind his business, or severe consequences could follow.

Due to overcrowded conditions, Eddie was again moved to yet another foster home near his seventh birthday. He knew it would be like all the others where people talked nice at you, but never really talked to you. People would say and do nice things without ever really meaning them. Usually they just gave orders and told you what you had to do in order to get along but never really cared about your point of view or about your plans or your dreams. He didn't know what love and caring felt like anymore, maybe he never had. His one hope was that there wouldn't be another Keith type person living at his new home.

Entering the new foster home, Eddie saw that this place was like a regular house. "Hi Eddie, I'm called Ms. Jan and I want you to meet my son, Jason; he's nine and Andrew who is also a foster child, just like you and he's eight years old. We want to welcome you here." As Eddie looked up into her face he realized that she was smiling and friendly and sounded truly happy that he was coming here to live. Still, he didn't trust the situation and would have to wait and see.

Then the back door opened and a man walked in. "Hi I'm Bill, they call me Mr. Bill here. I'm happy to meet you Eddie," he said and waited for a reply from Eddie. "Happy to meet you too," answered Eddie still feeling very suspicious of all this friendliness. He noticed that Mr. Bill wasn't very much taller than Ms. Jan. and he seemed to smile a lot too.

"Andrew is going to show you where to put your clothes since you'll be sharing a bedroom with him. I've got a job to finish outside and then I'll show you around the place and explain the rules, okay?" He waved and smiled again as he walked back out the door.

On the way to his bedroom, Andrew talked to Eddie. "I think you'll like it here. I didn't like my other foster homes at all, some were pretty bad, but the people here are pretty nice. It's more like a family. We do have rules to follow but they are pretty normal rules. Here we are; this is our bedroom. I have the bed on the right side and you can have that one over there. I've put all my stuff in the three dresser drawers on the right and you can have the three drawers on the left, okay?"

"Yes, but I don't have that much stuff."

"That's okay, but they're yours if you need them. I even put my school projects in the bottom drawer sometimes."

Looking around the room Eddie noticed a lot of posters on the wall, mostly of sports figures.

"Gees, you can have posters on the wall. That's neat," Eddie said as he looked longingly at the different ones that Andrew had collected.

"Who's your favorite? Andrew asked him.

"Oh, I like Magic Johnson. He wasn't very tall for a basketball player but he did great anyway. He's my role model 'cause I'm not tall either but I love to play."

"You know what, I think I might have a picture of him. I haven't put it up yet because my walls are pretty full. Do you want it?"

"Sure," said Eddie enthusiastically. "Do you think it

would be okay if I put it on my side of the room?"

"Yeah, of course, I would expect you to put it on your side. You sound like me when I first came here. But you'll see these people are really okay."

"How long have you been here?"

"Well, I made my rounds of several fosters homes. I think we both know how bad some can be, but I came here just after my sixth birthday and I didn't display many good manners and my attitude was awful. I'm embarrassed now as I look back but those other places, well, the older boys were always bullies and no one was around the keep them away. Oh, I can see by the look in your eyes that you've been to some of those too. Well, I know you have to find out like I did, but you did luck out coming here. You'll see."

Just then they heard their names being called for dinner and they both hurried downstairs.

"I heard that you like spaghetti and so tonight, in honor of your first evening here, I made it; I hope you like it," said Jan as she watched Eddie's eyes open wide.

"That's right," Jason said. "We all like spaghetti but tonight mom made it because you like it."

"Wow. Thanks," was all Eddie could manage to say in a very soft tone. With that they all sat down, gave blessings before dinner and Eddie proceeded to eat the best meal he had had in years. He almost cried tears because someone had done something just for him. What a great feeling that gave him. Then came dessert and the apple pie was scrumptious. For the first time in a long time, Eddie was very contented when he left the dinner table.

Mr. Bill took Eddie into his study room for a talk and to explain him the rules of the house. He seemed to be a lively man with dark brown hair having some gray showing through. He had a lot of enthusiasm for everything he talked about. He found fun in everything from breakfast to driving, and even to working.

"We're happy to have you here Eddie, and we hope you'll like us too. It looked like you enjoyed your dinner."

"Yes, Mr. Bill. That was a great dinner," said Eddie and he meant it. It was easy to be nice to Mr. Bill and Ms. Jan because they seemed to care about you. That was a new feeling for Eddie.

"Well, of course, like any other place, we do have some rules. We need to keep order in this household so everything runs smoothly, if you know what I mean?"

Eddie was almost sitting on the edge of his seat, anxiously awaiting to hear what he had to do. He wanted to do good here because so far, he liked it a lot.

"Here are the rules. You have to keep your room clean, make your bed every morning before school and make sure that you put your dirty clothes in the hamper. You have to clean up after yourself when you take a shower, and you have to take a shower every day. You also brush your teeth every day and you have to smell clean, except of course after exercise and then you take a shower. See how that works out. So far okay? Any questions."

"No, I don't think so. But I may have some later." Eddie wanted to leave the door open in case something came up later that he needed to understand.

"Okay, that's fine. Just a few more things. You have special clothes for school and other clothes to play in. Also, you have to help out me or Ms. Jan if we ask or need you. This probably seems like a lot of rules, right?" said Mr. Bill smiling.

"Yes, I hope I don't forget any." Eddie felt worried.

"Heh, lighten up Eddie. I don't expect you to remember everything the first day. We'll all help you and before long it'll be routine. You'll do fine. All you have to do is want to learn and you'll do just fine."

"Oh, I want to do good Mr. Bill; I really do."

"Then I'm sure you will. Any questions at all? No? Then I'll show you around the place. It isn't that big really but it's still fun for me. Okay?"

"Okay." And with that Mr. Bill showed Eddie the rest of the house and the basement that had a rather large recreation room with sports equipment and bikes. Mr. Bill was an engineer mainly but he coached basketball teams at the local school. Ms. Jan was a secretary for the school system. Eddie began to feel comfortable for the first time in years.

"Eddie, we don't know when your birthday is? We always celebrate birthdays here," asked Ms. Jan with her notebook in her hand.

"I don't know my birthday. Sorry." Eddie felt sad but also embarrassed. Most people knew their own birthday, but he didn't. Suddenly, he felt a hand on his shoulder. It was Mr. Bill. He had a habit of putting his hands on your shoulders when he was near you. He did it to all the boys and yet, it made Eddie feel special.

"Okay, Eddie. Do you remember anything at all about your birthday?"

"I think it was in July. But I don't know the date." Bill thought for a moment and asked, "What's your favorite number or your lucky number?" Eddie smiled. "I always like the number 17 for some reason. I really don't know why, but I like that number."

"Okay," said Bill with a mischievous wink, "July 17 it is. That's your birthday and we will celebrate that day just for you. Okay?" Eddie smiled at Bill and seemed happy as he nodded up and down. "Okay, I like that. July 17 it is."

As the months began to roll by, Eddie became very contented with his new foster home and hoped he would stay here until his mom caught up to him. It was the nicest place he had ever lived in and he really liked it, but he still thought about his mom. He was eight years old now and sometimes it was hard for him to remember what she looked like. He had forgotten her face a long time ago but he did have an impression and thought he remembered how she smelled. Yet time was passing and no one called; no one came.

"He really is a nice little boy, isn't he Bill? I shudder to think of what rough times he had at that last foster home." Jan looked at Bill for some insight.

"You know, Jan, it seems strange about Eddie. He just seemed to have materialized one day, without a past, without a history and became one of the statistics kids. There are so many of these kids with no real names, no real pasts, no life story that anyone knows about. They are society's question marks and what happens to them? They lead lives of confusion, distress and the courts scramble to ensure that they have some kind of chance at becoming well-adjusted." Bill stopped talking, almost suddenly.

"Yeah, I'm so glad that we have a chance to get some of them once in a while and make them feel special. They've got to know how important they are and some are so hard to convince."

"You know Jan, sometimes you can get caught up in all this and just want to take in a bunch of kids that you know aren't getting a real chance at life, but you and I can only do so much."

Just about this time the boys got home and it was time for dinner.

"Heh Eddie, I've got tomato soup to start us off. I know you like it a lot but do I overdo it or not?" asked Jan.

"Oh, no, Ms. Jan, I can never have too much tomato soup. Thanks," said Eddie laughing. Everyone thought it was good to see the positive change that had taken over his personality.

"Okay, you guys, how was school today?" asked Bill.

"I did good," answered Jason. "I did good," answered Andrew. "I did good," answered Eddie. Then they all looked at each other and laughed.

"I think I'm hearing some echoes in this room," said Bill. "Let's try this again. Is anyone having any problems at school?"

"No problems," answered Jason. "No problems," answered Andrew. "No problems," answered Eddie. Then they all laughed again, including Jan and Bill.

"I think I give up on all three of you, but I want you to know that Jan and I are doing good and we have no problems either." Everybody laughed and dinner that night was rather silly.

Months turned into years and luckily Eddie remained at this foster home. By grades 7 and 8 he joined Junior Varsity basketball now and was tall enough at 5'7" to be considered a forward, although he liked playing point guard. He moved very well and was quick and agile. Coaches and scouts were thinking Eddie might be a good recruit next year for Thurston High. The assistant coach George Bowers (the officer from the police station) had already talked to Bill about Eddie's potential.

"That kid of yours can really move, can't he? I almost forget some of the time that he really isn't the fastest runner on this team," mentioned George as they both watched a game where Eddie was particularly agile.

"Yeah, he thinks so fast on his feet. I've talked to him about it and he says he just uses his gut feeling. And you can't get better than that." Bill had spent some time working with Eddie, especially when he'd first come to live with them. "He's always loved basketball and from the first time he saw that hoop on our garage door he felt he had a place to practice. I played with him a lot too and so did the others. Then when he made the Junior Varsity on his first try, well, we had one happy little guy in our house."

"Yes, he's come a long way, hasn't he?" said George happily.

"Yeah, his luck has changed and it's great to watch him grow, you know?"

As luck would have it, Eddie graduated from Grade 8 and made the team at Thurston High the very next year, just as predicted. He still had only a few friends, and they were mostly the basketball players but they all connected well. Eddie didn't trust people very much, but there was an exception with his foster parents. If Eddie was beginning to trust anyone at all, it was Bill and Jan, and possibly his two brothers.

"You should be feeling pretty good about yourself these days," said Bill teasingly. "You played a terrific game last night and passed your 9<sup>th</sup> Grade algebra. Good day for you, buddy." Bill said this as he stood behind Eddie and put his hands on his shoulders. Bill still did that and Eddie still liked it. He liked that slight personal contact, but still got embarrassed if Jan hugged him, and she did.

"Well, you know Bill, I work hard on basketball all the time and I worked myself crazy studying algebra but what the heck the end justified the means, right?"

Eddie turned and looked at Bill for a long moment. At the end of Grade 9, just two months from now, they all planned to take a one-week vacation, destination to be decided by the entire family. Eddie stood there, thinking how lucky life had turned out for him. The family had already adopted Andrew and his foster family planned on keeping him too. The paperwork was already in progress but it was painfully slow. Neither his mother nor his father had ever showed up so their parental rights were terminated by the time Eddie was twelve. But looking into Bill's face he knew that, at least, this family wanted him and he really did have a mom and a dad. Until the paperwork came through, this was okay with him and Eddie felt that he had found a happy life.

Then tragedy struck. Again nothing was permanent in Eddie's life. The foster home of Jan and Bill Conrad caught fire and although never proven, arson was suspected. Mr. Bill died of smoke inhalation, Ms. Jan survived but suffered serious lung damage. Luckily, the children escaped unharmed. After her initial recovery, Jan planned to recuperate in Indiana living with her sister, and she was taking her son Jason and her adopted child Andrew. Since Eddie was not officially adopted, the legal system wouldn't let him go. Eddie was taken and placed in another foster home on the other side of town that totally disrupted his life. Other than the obvious grieving he would do, he had to attend another school, make new friends, new social workers, in other words, he had to start all over again. This was the third time in his life he had to completely start over and Eddie Sabers was only fourteen years old.

Eddie did have a chance to talk to Jan, Jason and Andrew before they left to move to another state. Almost everyone cried a least a little and Jan was so angry and sad for not being able to take Eddie, but it was the legal system.

"Soon you'll be 18 and then you can come and live with us," Jan said. "We'll always want you with us and we'll miss you so much."

"I'll be fine," Eddie told her. He knew that Jan was not well. The smoke had damaged her lungs badly and the prognosis still wasn't definite on her.

"You know, this has been a great seven years, the best of my entire life. Sometimes, when I'm sad, I'll just remember us sitting around the kitchen table laughing at Bill's more than corny jokes until my stomach hurt. Nobody will ever take those moments away from me." Eddie wanted to say something important; anything that would make a difference to Jan because he knew her life had collapsed in more ways than one.

As he gave Jan a final hug, he made it real long because he wanted to remember her, how she felt, how she smelled and how he felt safe and content when she was around. Then he actually hugged Jason and Andrew. Usually the boys didn't hug each other, but they did that day.

"I'll always think of you guys as brothers," said Eddie with tears falling and loving feelings coming from his heart.

"And we'll always love you like a brother," they said fighting tears.

"Life is just crappy sometimes; first dad and now you can't come with us. Life just sucks. Nothing will ever be the same," said Jason who surprised Eddie with a show of emotion. "I never told you I love you Eddie, but I do and I'm glad you came to live with us. I just can't imagine you not being around," he continued in an angry tone.

"Soon, I will live wherever I want when I'm eighteen in

four more years, and who knows?" said Eddie thinking wishfully about the future.

"I love you too," said Andrew, "and I don't think it's fair. You didn't do anything wrong or bad." There was so much anger and sadness going around.

"We'll all have to be positive," Eddie reminded the other two. "Bill would have a fit listening to all of us talk this way. He would give us all very bad consequences, don't you think?"

"I know you're right Eddie," said Jan, "and we'll all have to remember that Bill will always be with each one of us forever in our hearts, in our spirits and in our face if we start to goof off." Everyone laughed in remembrance of Bill's firm attitude.

"How is your present foster home?" asked Jan. "Are they nice over there?"

"It's okay, really, don't worry Jan. I'll be fine. It's not the Conrad home but it's only for a few more years. I'm doing okay." Eddie hoped that he kept his concern hidden. He lapsed into memory and thought, *Why did Bill have to die? I just learned to depend on someone and now it will be much harder than before I knew what it was like when someone cared.* He couldn't tell Jan. She had enough on her plate. He couldn't tell Jason and Andrew either; they didn't need to feel any worse. There were too many children at this new foster home, not enough food and too few caregivers. The bullies were still there as when he'd been a small child. He had already gotten into trouble just trying to stop an older kid from beating up one of the younger ones and he was learning to keep to himself again. He hated living in this foster home and mostly he hated being moved around all of the time. Mr. Bill was constantly on his mind as was the rest of his family that he had to let go. Eddie watched as they started getting into the van and he still watched as the van pulled away and turned the corner. He lingered and stared. He just didn't want this part of his life to end. Not today; not ever.

"Let's go Eddie," said his escort. The words shocked him back to reality and made him realize he was really alone again, just like before, and now it was back to that foster home.

"Yeah, okay Sam." He was grateful that Sam, one of the caregivers, had agreed to drive him so he could at least say goodbye to his family.

"I know it's not the best place but they do feed you and you have a roof over your head. But I know there are real problems there." Eddie had to agree that Sam had made some good points.

"Yeah, but it's the little ones that really suffer, don't they? I've tried to help but I just get myself into trouble, so I quit."

"Heh, you were little in foster homes, weren't you? I guess you understand what the little ones are going through." Sam was thinking out loud but Eddie knew that he realized.

"I wish I could help them but I can't even help myself right now. Just wish I could though."

"Well, Eddie, maybe someday you will. And maybe someday someone may help you."

"Can't imagine that but I guess it's a nice thought."

"Well, Eddie, you never know about life. Really, kid, you just never know."

# Chapter Two

Time passed on and found Eddie mostly a loner. By the age of sixteen he found himself reflecting many times about his life. He couldn't play basketball anymore since he had to be on the bus to and from school, which didn't allow time for practice. He was usually rude in class, had an unpleasant tone for adults and just a nasty outlook on life. He knew Mr. Bill wouldn't be proud of him, but he couldn't help it. He realized he had to finish high school but he couldn't keep his anger under control. Everything about his life was unfair and he couldn't understand why God was against him, if there really was a God. He was jealous of everyone with a good family life and didn't care anymore. Everything good in his life kept leaving. He often wondered why he didn't have any permanence in his life?

Eddie had gotten suspended from high school twice and with an extra warning he could get expelled any day. The foster home didn't want children who were expelled from school because the state lowered their income. This foster home didn't want children in their home to take care of them; they just wanted the money the children brought in.

"Where the hell have you been?" asked the unpleasant voice of Nina, one of the group home caregivers. Eddie looked at her as she stood on the porch, hair uncombed, ugly yellow teeth, dirty clothes, smoking a cigarette. She didn't really care where Eddie had been; it was just a nosy question. She would only care if he didn't come back and she lost money.

"Just around, that's all." Eddie answered because he wasn't up to one of her interrogation sessions. He knew that Nina loved to torment him, as well as the other kids.

"Around where and keep your manners when you address me, you punk," she yelled back.

"Just around walking, nowhere really," he answered back.

"Well just see to it that you are here tomorrow at 6:00 PM when the social worker comes and be on good behavior too. I want no mention of John punching you yesterday since he was kind of drunk so it doesn't count. If you want food for the next couple of days, you'll forget it."

"Yeah, right," Eddie answered. He didn't really care. He didn't spend much time here anyway, just when he needed sleep and got hungry. Usually there was something to eat and he had heard about other group homes that were much worse with real crazies living there. He thought Nina was sort of crazy herself but he could handle her and the other kids were usually gone most of the time, unless it was time for the social worker. Then they all came in and said the right things and acted in the right way. All the kids got rewarded for a while if Nina was happy. And that is how Eddie's life played out for a while. Others had similar stories, true, with only the circumstances and scenarios different but the results were usually the same.

In the courtroom, people began moving around as the hour drew near for the cases to be heard. The hustle and bustle in the room brought Eddie back to the present moment.

Eddie shivered as he shifted nervously in his seat

waiting for the judge to arrive. Yet, there was nothing he could do but wait. Thinking back he remembered how his depression had deepened when he'd started hanging around with Joe Mucci and Tim Harrington. They both had affluent families and liked to take serious risks. It was almost fun at the beginning and the first excitement he'd had in his life in a long time. He knew their activities were dangerous but he thought money would help to solve his problems. Eddie agreed to steel hub caps. It was easy and he actually had enough money to buy himself a new shirt and then he had a steak dinner. But along with all this came a bad attitude where Eddie just didn't care about himself or anyone else. He got into more fights at school and finally got expelled. Nina made it so unpleasant that he left and lived on the street for a while. Then came the drug deal. He hated the thought of it but he was so hungry. He knew the danger was high and on the third trip out, they were caught.

"Eddie Sabers, let's go," said the guard.

Eddie picked up his stuff and got up when he was supposed to and faced His Honor. The judge had a reputation for being fair but when there was no one to stand up with you, no one to help when you hit bottom, there wasn't much for a person to do.

"Eddie Sabers, what are we going to do with you? Is there anyone here for you?" asked the judge.

"No, your Honor," answered Eddie.

"Is there anyone you want to call to post bail or to confer with?" the judge asked again.

"No, your Honor, there is no one," said Eddie.

"This is a serious offense, young man. I've only seen you once before in my court and it was a minor offense, but you haven't straightened out and you're still going in the wrong direction. You're charged with drug possession. You need someone here – don't you have any family, someone you could call?" asked the judge again with heartfelt concern.

"There's no one your Honor," repeated Eddie. He just hated to hear himself say those words but there was just no one – no one at all.

"Well, I'm going to give you a few moments to think real hard because if there's no one here to post bail and no one to speak for you, then you'll be staying in jail. Now, I know that's not what you want, is it?" Eddie felt that the judge was looking for another solution as he had told him before that many of the kids just needed someone to guide them along. He knew some were desperate but that one person could sometimes make a big difference in a person's life. So the judge waited and gave Eddie more time.

Eddie was thinking with all the brainpower he ever had and nothing was coming forward. There was no one. There had hardly ever been anyone for him in his whole entire miserable life and there would never be. Now for sure, there would never be. He wanted to scream it out as loud as he could so all the world would hear. THERE'S NO ONE WHO CARES FOR EDDIE SABERS. But he remained silent and angry within. He just stood there and waited.

"Well, I have to do something with you. You've been in the holding cell for two nights. I suppose I'll have to transfer you to a juvenile home and get you a court appointed lawyer. With no bail, and no one to take responsibility for you, you'll have to go to a juvenile home." The judge said this very slowly allowing time to let it sink into Eddie's mind and because he wished there was an alternative.

"So ordered," said the judge and just as his gavel was coming down there was a voice at the back of the courtroom that yelled out, "Can I speak, Your Honor? I'll post bail. I'll be responsible for Eddie Sabers. May I address the court?"

The scene seemed like something right out of a Perry Mason movie as everyone in the courtroom turned around quickly, in unison, to put a face on the voice from the back of the room. Standing up was a single figure of a middle-aged man of average height and build with dark hair, speckled with a lot of silver. He was dressed casually and had a pleasant though bland look on his face which made it totally impossible to read his expression.

Eddie was numb. Before he had a chance to turn around his mind went racing wildly. That voice, that voice was so familiar. He knew that voice from somewhere. As he turned around with everyone else to see who could possibly be doing this, his heart skipped a funny beat. Who would be willing to put up bail money for him and why? Eddie stared at the neat figure of a man he hadn't seen or heard of in almost four years. This was a man he had only known slightly in the past and Eddie wondered how he could have even known about him and his present trouble. Why would he be doing this?

"Come forward sir," said the judge. "You are willing to post bail for Eddie Sabers?"

"Yes sir, I will post bail for Eddie Sabers," replied George in a firm and determined voice.

Staring directly at the face of George Bowers as he searched his memory, Eddie had a moment of recollection. He thought he remembered seeing him standing with Mr. Bill at a few of the basketball games. Sure, he was a friend of Mr. Bill and Eddie thought he may have been at the house a few times. George wasn't even one of the main coaches, but just there in the background taking orders from John Agin. Rumor said that John was not a great man to work with and was very tough on all of his assistance coaches, yelling and screaming at them for bad times, yet taking all the glory for good times, but George always came and helped out. But then Mr. Agin fell out of favor with the school administrator and was let go right near the last two weeks of the season and George had taken over their team. That was the only reason Eddie even remembered him.

"That is only the first part. Eddie is a minor at sixteen, so you would have to take personal responsibility for him. He also has no place to live so you would have to give him shelter. That would be at least through the court case or until he's eighteen years old and depending on the outcome, well, we would see. Now sir, are you willing to do all that for this young sixteen year old whose suspected of dealing drugs and stealing?" The judge stared at George searching his face, while waiting for an answer.

"Yes, your honor, I am willing to do that for Eddie." This was not answered quickly but slowly and very deliberately.

"May I ask why sir? How do you know this boy? I want you to realize what you're taking on." The judge was very serious in wanting to know the real reason for this bit of generosity.

"Well, your honor, I knew this child when he was in the 7th Grade. I was one of his basketball coaches and he was a good point guard back then." *Of course*, thought Eddie, *I was right. He was at those basketball games. He was a friend of Mr. Bill.* George continued, "He had a tough young life but he got into a good foster home and he was doing nicely at that time. I'd like to see him become that way again and I think he could if he got a chance. I'd like to give him that chance, your Honor." George said this with empathy and sincerity and Eddie felt a lump starting to develop in his throat.

123

"Okay sir, you seem to know him pretty well. But he has changed a lot and you should know that you would be responsible if I sign him out to your custody. He just recently turned sixteen." The judge waited to be sure that George really understood. George did understand and there was something else that the judge wasn't aware of.

Once in a casual conversation, Bill had asked George to be Eddie's friend if anything ever happened to him. Bill was pleased with Eddie's progress but he realized that it had to do with stability and structure in his life and also because Eddie now was sure that someone really cared for him. George had told Bill that he would be happy to watch out for Eddie so now George was fulfilling a promise to a friend.

"Yes, your honor, I understand and I'm willing to take on that responsibility."

Turning to Eddie, the Judge emphasized his thoughts. "You're one lucky young man, Eddie Sabers, to have someone come forward for you. Take this chance and go with it and listen to this man. He has much to teach you about life, living and learning to care for others. You'll have to be back in court for your trial and we don't know what will happen at that time, but your chances sure look better than they did thirty minutes ago. Take advantage of it."

"So ordered," said the judge and this time the gavel came all the way down to his desk to give that eerie sound of finality.

Eddie turned to face George, whom he hadn't seen in such a long time. He wanted to tell him how much he appreciated what he was doing, but he didn't. He wanted to say how much he missed Bill, as he knew George did, but he didn't. He wanted to ask him why he was doing this for him and how lousy he felt about the last few years, but he didn't. But he knew he had to say something.

"Thanks Mr. Bowers, I don't know what to say," was all he could manage with a very meek smile and then he quickly looked down at the floor trying to hide his embarrassment. George paid the bail and as they walked out together there was only silence between them. There was so much to say but the silence between them was louder than words.

When they reached the car, George said, "Are you hungry, Eddie? I'd love to get something to eat. Courtrooms always give me an appetite."

Eddie nodded yes and began to say something again about how much he appreciated what George had done for him but was immediately cut off.

"Later Eddie, we've lots of time later but for now, let's just forget everything and enjoy some food and the happy memories you and I shared during that 7$^{th}$ Grade basketball season with our mutual friend Bill."

Settling in at the Knight's Inn, Eddie looked around at the décor. It was pretty simple in some ways, basically decorated around old-fashioned items of past years. But it did give one a feeling of solid background and dependability. Eddie liked that.

"That was quite a season we had didn't we? Did you play forward or point guard back then? I don't remember." George was trying to get Eddie talking but it was tough at first. Slowly, though he began reminiscing along with George.

"You know, I was mainly a forward but sometimes Mr. Bill put me as a point guard. I think I liked that position the best. You know, Mr. Bowers, I don't really know what to call you. Mr. Bowers, Mr. George or what?"

"You're sixteen now and I think you can call me George, okay? I want to tell you that they've got the best ground round hamburgers here that I've ever had. That's what I usually order. You can have whatever."

"I like them too." So when the waitress came the order was placed and all that came with it.

"You played real well. I remember you, you know why?"

"No, why?" Eddie wondered.

"Bill and I used to talk about it. You weren't the tallest player we had and height does help a lot in basketball. But you moved so well and you were fast thinking on your feet."

"Bill used to talk to me about that. It wasn't anything I planned but I had what I called quick gut feelings and just went with them." George could see by Eddie's expressions and responses that many moments of pride were covering his mind and creeping out of a long buried areas of his memory.

"Yeah, but you were a natural. You know, a guy can be tall and even move fast but if he doesn't have those natural instincts, well, he can still be hampered. You were quite good." George knew exactly what he was doing. As a semi-retired policeman, it pained him to see what happened to many children who were abandoned or dreadfully neglected. George took special interest in these children and he worked well with troubled teens. And, of course, Eddie was special to him. He had been at the police station the night Eddie was brought in as a frightened four year old. "Yeah, you weren't the fastest runner we had but you were the best mover on the court," George reminded him.

"Seems like a long time ago," said Eddie as present day problems crossed his face.

"Yeah, sad that good things seem to come to an end. But there's always more good ahead."

126

Eddie didn't seem very convinced but added. "These hamburgers are the best. I have to agree with you about that." Talking about happier times had brightened his spirits and gave him a hint of hope.

On the ride home George had started a conversation a few times and realized that Eddie was nodding off. He figured that he probably hadn't gotten much sleep the last few nights so he didn't awaken him. George remembered back to some conversations he'd had with Bill.

"I'm so proud of Eddie. How far that kid has come, George. Honestly you wonder how he made it, inside you know. He was so depressed, scared and just an inward child when I first got him. So unsure of himself and he was a real loner. He only depended on himself."

"Yeah, that's what happens when nothing is permanent in your life. Most kids that I saw were in trouble because of being abandoned and neglected. That's such a tough feeling and you know, Bill, I really can't imagine believing inside that no one cares for you. Imagine thinking no one loves you and you can't trust anyone."

"Who could live like that? Who would want to?" said Bill rather alone for a moment in his thoughts. George looked over at Bill and realized that they were sharing silent beliefs.

"The suicide rate for these kids is so high. Life is worth nothing to them; no one cares and they have no hope." George added these comments from memories in his past as a cop. He had seen a lot of hopeless kids, of all ages.

"I think this is what happened to Eddie," continued Bill. "Two things really. Slowly he started to have hope and then he started to trust us. It took a lot of time and a stop and go process but finally it began. We were consistent in our parenting which is real important and we thought enough of him to give him consequences for bad behavior."

"Funny, isn't it? These kids need limits and someone to make sure they stay inside the limits. Even when you know they're mad at you and even hate you at times, inside they know you care. Life is funny that way."

"Well, Eddie finally started believing in himself because we believed in him too. What a thrill seeing some kid start to grow and soar in the right direction. I always showed him how I appreciated it when he did a good job. It's the little things George."

"The little things aren't really so little. They're just one block at a time and they keep growing. Just being there day after day and not leaving and showing Eddie you really care, that must have been it." George knew how consistency had helped his life.

"And the other boys – they cared about him too. We all became a family. Who would have thought?"

"Great feeling huh?" said George who liked being a part of it all.

"Yeah, we have started proceedings to adopt Eddie. Just a formality really but then he will feel he belongs here permanently."

"That's great Bill."

"George, if anything should ever happens to me, would you look out for Eddie and the others, but especially Eddie? He's the youngest and was alone for so long. You've had so much experience in your police work and he'd need someone strong."

"Heh Bill, you mean you're a mere mortal being?"

George teased.

"Yeah, I know, but just in case. What do you say? I've been lax at putting things down on paper but I just want to be sure."

"Sure I would. I love Eddie too. What a great example he is. He will be such a good role model to other kids because he understands. You and I can have empathy with other kids, you know, and we try to help them. But Eddie can say, "I know how you feel." You and I can't do that. However, I hope that sometime in the not too distance future, you'll be inviting me to his college graduation and I want to tell you now that of course, I'll be there."

And that was how some of their conversations went. George thought about Bill at this moment on the highway, with Eddie asleep next to him, and told him that he would do the best he could for Eddie and hoped that Bill would contribute guidance from wherever he was. He felt satisfied with his life as he drove along quietly, remembering yesterday morning, as he was having a leisurely cup of coffee and enjoying his day off until the newspaper was delivered and he first heard about Eddie's latest troubles.

He had been staring at the non-fruit pear tree out of his patio door. He remembered planting that tree over to the left side of his yard, just a little shrub at the time, but now it was in full bloom casting its shadow all the way to the neighbor's patio. He loved that tree with its beautiful white foliage and straight tender trunk that belied its strength to withstand the frigid winter cold as well as the much larger trees. People could be like that, he thought, some of the seemingly tender and meek ones withstood so many adversities that they could stand tall next to anyone. Funny the way life could be.

George had thought of himself that way, strong and tough and weathered throughout his life. He had always been on the small side with his stature ending at five feet seven inches, not tall for a man. That had put him in a category to be bullied as a child, but his quick wit always outsmarted his adversaries. Five foot seven wasn't tall for a policeman either, yet he managed to survive some very difficult assignments on his cleverness and quickness of thought alone. He felt life was fair and always gave compensations in its life plan.

"George, honey, I need your help. Can you come in here a moment?"

That was Lisa, his wife of twenty-five years – his other self as he called her. She was packing away some blankets for next winter and always needed his help stacking the boxes on the shelf.

"Coming dear," answered George in his usual teasing tone that let Lisa think he was just there for her every whim. He admired her and felt always that he had made a good choice of partners.

"Can you hold this box while I get the other one?" she asked.

"Why don't you just get the other box and I'll put them both up for you?" he suggested and felt satisfaction as he saw her grateful smile.

George never understood why Lisa didn't just ask him to do these jobs in the first place since the final result was always the same. Yet that was probably what he liked most about Lisa, her willingness to attempt difficult tasks.

"Thanks dear," which is always the way their helping sessions ended. He looked at his petite blonde blue-eyed wife and realized she solidly contrasted with his dark hair and dark eyes. Their personalities complemented each other with Lisa as the cautious, practical one to George's happy-go-lucky, fun loving demeanor. She was already a registered nurse when she'd met George, a rookie cop. They had lived a good life together with only one regret – no children. They discussed adopting once or twice but the timing was never right with George's unpredictable hours at the precinct and Lisa's mostly rotating shifts in nursing.

"George, have you talked to the shelter for boys lately. I've noticed they had another ad in the paper the other day."

"I'm going on another special assignment soon, but maybe after that I'll check with them."

"Yeah, you love it so. But then you're still coaching basketball for Varsity, right? How much longer will that last?"

"Actually, next week will be the finals and then I'm done for this year." George thought about all the kids he had met and some he had helped in the years gone by. Underneath his policeman training was a guy with many classes and seminars regarding troubled youths. He seemed to connect very well with the children of society. Officers from the precinct and teachers and parents from the area schools sought George's help since he seemed to have an uncanny savvy as to what was going on inside these kids.

Sitting down again to read his newspaper, George was shocked at what he saw in the headlines. "I can't believe this, I can't believe this. Lisa, Lisa – look at this front page."

George's eyes had caught the story about three teenagers who got busted for drug possession. He had read quickly through the article as Lisa walked back into the kitchen.

"Oh no, gees, oh no," cried George in an angry, desperate and very agitated tone.

"George, what's wrong?" He felt Lisa's presence near him.

"Oh no, damn it. I knew something was going to happen. Damn it."

"George?" yelled Lisa. George heard her concern but was still in such angry shock that he was still into himself.

"You remember Eddie Sabers, that kid that lived with Bill and Jan. He just got arrested on a drug bust."

"Oh no," she said as George watched her jaw drop open.

They both stood there and stared at each other and then stared at the headlines for a few more minutes in disbelief. George felt that he had suddenly lost his energy, so he took a long deep breath and let it out slowly to gain time in recovering his composure. He was hurt deeply and Lisa shared his pain as they thought about Eddie's life and disgust at this turn of events.

George stammered. "Gees, I'm really pissed off at this. We could have made a difference. We really could have made a difference and damn that court system that put him in that crappy foster home instead of letting us take him. They should rot for this. I was pretty sure it was just a matter of time."

Lisa added, "How sad George, how very sad."

"I tried to watch out for him anyway, Lisa, you know that, but it was just hands off. We sure do have crazy rules for caring for these kids."

"It wasn't fair, George. We could have taken him when Bill died."

"I guess a cop and a nurse just wasn't good enough for these courts and they put him in that awful foster home. Honestly Lisa, most homes are okay, look at Bill and Jan, but that one where they sent Eddie had a real bad reputation and they still didn't shut it down. I'm really pissed off. Sorry honey."

"I could swear myself," said Lisa, "this is just so unfair."

"Right honey, you could just swear." At that comment George had to smile in spite of the seriousness of the situation. Despite his disappointment, the idea of Lisa letting go with a line of swearing was amusing to him.

"Just a figure of speech George. This is all so stupid. We could have helped that boy."

"Maybe we still can. He'd blossomed into such a good kid under Bill and Jan's tutoring. I felt he could really make it. I still do."

"What do you mean, maybe we still can? What are you thinking?"

"You see, at that time he had someone who cared about him and he knew it. That was really the first time in his life someone cared for him. What a difference that had made."

"It would make a difference in anyone's life."

"He did get involved with drugs though, passing them on I think, not using from what I can tell. Probably needed money real bad because it says he had been living on the streets the last few months. Kicked out of that foster home. Oh see here hon," George read on in the article, "Eddie was expelled from school, doesn't say why, but I bet you the foster home loses money if you're not in school so they threw him out for another kid who was in school."

"My word, George. Eddie's story really makes a person want to cry."

"Or to do something about it. He can make it Lisa; I just

know it. I saw a hopeful kid a while back. And, oh yeah, remember what Bill used to say, 'This kid will be one great role model someday.' If he'd stayed with Bill, he'd have done just fine."

"Yeah, I think you're right. And then Jan wasn't allowed to take him with her so that means he lost a dad and a mother and two brothers. And they moved away so far, which didn't help either."

"The cards are stacked against him right now. Remember the last letter from Jan, she said she had only heard from him once and she was worried. How can we tell her this?"

"How indeed George. Well, it must be our time. What do you have in mind?"

"What? What makes you think I have anything in mind?"

"G-e-o-r-g-e." He heard Lisa say his name slowly and drag out every syllable. "We've been married twenty-five years come October. Now what do you have in mind?"

"Let me make my call first."

After the call, George carefully returned the receiver to its cradle and then walked slowly back into the kitchen. He had a plan coming up from deep inside of him and he wanted to fulfill it but he wondered and hoped Lisa would agree. It would never work without Lisa's full and complete agreement. Was it too much to ask of her?

"And?"

"His arraignment in court is tomorrow. If he has no one there for him to post bail, he'll go to juvenile detention until his trial. That's not good, believe me. And it doesn't seem that he has anyone there for him. He must feel as low as can be and so alone."

"Well, George, I guess you'll have to go get him then, won't you?"

George couldn't believe his ears. He was shaken out of his thoughts momentarily by the exact intuitiveness of his wife who knew him so well. He was still trying to figure out how present this idea to Lisa, and she had already said yes.

"Lisa, how did you know I was going to ask that?"

G-e-o-r-g-e," said Lisa in the same drawn out fashion of pronouncing his name, "we've been married twenty-five years come October ..."

"Okay, okay." George laughed and shook his head slowly as he cut her off.

"So what do you have in mind if you are finally ready to tell me?"

"Well, I want to post bail. But understand honey, he's been living on the streets and the judge won't allow that."

"Right, so he moves in with us and then what?" She said this last statement like it was a forgone conclusion anyway.

George got up to come around and give Lisa the biggest and longest hug he had given her in a very long time.

"I'm so glad I married you Lisa."

"Okay, George, that's nice. But what do you have in mind for Eddie?"

"It's not all in place yet, but first I thought we could give him a home, you know, not just a house to live in. He has to know someone cares about him. I want to work with him a lot – plans aren't all solid in my mind yet, but just get him back in school, and see if we can find and bring out that great role model Bill talked about. We might have some rough times for a while so we have to be in this together. If you want to think about it, I understand."

"I'm with you George, and besides, how could I live with you if we didn't take him in? I've always thought you should have been a social worker anyway. Maybe now you are, a part-time cop and the part-time social worker. Either way, I'm with you George. I always am."

"I know you are hon, and Eddie needs to see again what life can be like."

With his plan in motion, George called the precinct to get all of the details on Eddie and scheduled to be in court by 10: A.M. the next day.

It was sad to see Eddie standing alone before the judge, looking so depressed and lost. He had heard Eddie say twice that he had no one to post bail for him. That would have to be the absolute bottom when you have no one to stand by you when you need friends or family. So that made a proud moment for George Bowers as he stood up in the back of the courtroom to say he would post bail. A very proud moment indeed.

As they walked out of the courtroom, Eddie began, "I don't know how to thank you. I mean we barely know each other ..."

Before the drive was half-way over, Eddie suddenly woke up. Conversation was still somewhat strained between the two of them but the earlier discussion about Bill and the basketball games eased the tension somewhat. Eddie thought, *I feel like I should be talking very nice and very appreciatively to George but I just can't seem to do it. I'm just sitting here, like an idiot. Gee, it's nice to be riding in a car again, especially when I could still be sitting in jail or going to juvenile. And that could still happen. And it would be well deserved. How stupid I've been lately, how crappy life is anyway.*

Eddie's thoughts were not clear. As hard as he tried to start a plan in his mind, it seemed like there was no energy left inside of him. His brain was all mixed up. Early memories came back to him about feeling mixed up. *I keep thinking about my mom. How could she just leave me at that playground and never come back? Not even a phone call.* These were not clear precise memories and truthfully, they never had been. It was more like an impression that was left on his mind, all dark and somehow lost in the shadows, but the remembrance could sometimes bring on a bout of depression. He had fought it for years. Many times he thought he had lost it, but it always seemed to find him again. It was as if a dark cloud came over him at times and try as he may, he couldn't escape it. That dark cloud had been around constantly since Bill Conrad died and it always brought up an anger and pain that affected all his thinking and all of this moods. Life had been in turmoil for him for a very long time.

George tried to make conversation. "This is lovely country around here. Makes me feel good just to drive it sometimes."

"Yeah it is," answered Eddie. And that's all he said. He knew he wasn't being nice but he had no idea what to say. What was expected of him? God, what was he supposed to do? He knew he had a jail term facing him. His spirits took a downward turn again. He was thinking that maybe he should break the silence this time, but what should he say?

Eddie snuck a peek at George as he was driving. He

barely remembered him and thought he liked him. He didn't have any bad feelings about him or actually, no feelings one way or the other. He mostly remembered him talking to Bill at basketball, although he thought George might have come to their home once or twice. It was a long time ago. He figured he probably liked him because Bill liked him and back then he usually liked what Bill liked. Bill had awakened in him a feeling of belonging to someone in this world and that feeling gave him considerable motivation. But it had disappeared after Bill died. Eddie felt again that he should make an attempt at conversation. The destination was still about forty-five minutes away from what he'd been told and he guessed talking might be easier now than later.

"George, I can't believe you're doing this for me. Why? I can't pay you back."

"I really didn't want to see you in jail Eddie."

"Oh. How did you hear about it?

"It was in all the papers."

"Oh yeah, right. Who could miss those huge headlines."

"Was a pretty big story round here. Want to talk about it?"

Eddie felt somewhat reckless. "I passed out some drugs and got caught. Sucks to be me."

"Why Eddie?"

"Why not? Fast money." Eddie didn't know why some words were coming out of him. He sounded so flippant, but he didn't feel that way.

"Have you ever used drugs?"

"That stupid I'm not. Don't use, just passed them on."

"Think that's a good profession for you?"

Eddie was silent for a long moment. He really was talking rude and nasty to George. Why? George had just done him a huge favor. He could even take off running and never have to face that judge again.

"I got kicked out of school, you know. I won't ever get a profession."

"What happened?"

"Eight of us got into a big fight – don't matter why, there's always something to fight about. But I was the only one who got expelled."

"How come?"

"I was the only one that didn't have anyone to fight for me. Those other boys had parents who couldn't get to the school fast enough dancing around the principal and offering to donate to things, you know. Sounded like a bribe to me."

"Do you think it was fair?"

"What? That I got expelled? Probably, I really deserved it but so did the others. Like I said, it sucks to be me."

"What would you like to do now Eddie?"

"Don't know. Don't really care." Eddie did it again. He was acting like a jerk and couldn't seem to force himself to talk respectfully.

"If you did care, what would you like to do?"

Finally Eddie's arrogance let up a little and he got quiet

for quite a while. Finally he answered. "I'd like to go back in time."

"To when?"

"I'd like to bring Bill back and those years that I lived with him and his family. I really miss him."

"Yeah, I'll bet Jan and the boys would do that too if they could."

"I still think about them often. You knew them, right? Did you ever keep in touch? Sometimes I wonder how they're doing?"

"Jan wrote us about two years ago. She was worried about you and said she hadn't heard from you."

"Yeah, well I just decided to cut all ties. Know what I mean?"

He saw George shake his head in acknowledgement. He figured he knew that he liked to keep his distance. After that last comment, Eddie got lost in his own thoughts the rest of the way home.

It took a few days for Eddie to get used to the routine of the home. It was the usual, pick up after yourself, clean up your sink and shower after use, make your bed and as far as laundry, you could do your own or you could combine it with George and Lisa. Dinner was served at a certain time and people ate together with no arguments – only positive happy things. Breakfast and lunch were your own choice. There was always food around and it was for everyone. It was a good plan and Eddie fell into step very quickly.

Lisa and George had decided they would have to take a chance and see what Eddie would do with someone trusting him. Would Eddie steal, run away, try moving drugs again?

140

No one knew. George felt Eddie wouldn't do the drug scene again. It was just a feeling. Stealing and running away, he wasn't sure. He wanted to give him a few more days to think about his life and what he wanted to do before forcing any issues.

"Eddie, Lisa and I aren't going to always be around here 24/7. We're always in and out. Lisa's a nurse and gets assignments and I still work part-time as a cop. We've decided we're going to trust you. There's a lot here to steal, if you decide and you'd have a good chance of just taking off too. I couldn't stop you even if I was here, even I know that."

"Why are you telling me this. Trying to set me up?"

"No, oh no. I just want you to know and realize how it is."

"What do you want of me? Why did you do this?"

"Right now, I would like to see you take some time, a few more days or so and just think about your life and what you'd like to do with it."

"I'm going to jail George, remember? I'm just out on bail right now."

"You never know, Eddie. You've got three months before your trial. If the judge sees a kid who is trying to do right, well, you never know. And you're only sixteen. You could get a break – maybe, maybe not."

"Right," said Eddie with a haughty laugh, "me get a break."

"Maybe your time has come to get lucky. Anyway, think about things. This place is your home for now. Read, watch TV, take walks, do whatever but at the end of the week, we'll talk again, or sooner if you want."

"How can I think about what I'm gonna do? I did some real stupid things and I'm going to jail."

"Look at it this way Eddie, if you weren't going to jail, what do you think you'd like to do?"

"Seems crazy to me."

"Just give it a try and see what you come up with."

"George, just one question."

"Yeah, what?"

"Well, um, um…"

"What Eddie?"

"Why did you do this for me?"

Eddie saw George smile at him as he looked into his eyes and said, "Because I think you're worth it."

With that George turned and walked out of the room and closed the door and left Eddie just standing there in disbelief. Eddie found it hard to believe that George still believed in him and the tone of his voice had a richness all its own.

In his room Eddie lay down on his bed, stretching his legs out as far as he could in complete comfort and put his hands behind his head as he looked up at the ceiling. Just a few days ago, he was looking at the ceiling in a jail cell. He was still dazed by the activities of the last week. His life was a mess and he was just too emotionally exhausted to even try to think. He was sure in the back of his mind were some clear thoughts but he had no energy right now to move them forward, nor did he want to. He was in a daze and wanted to stay there. Tomorrow he had to begin creating a plan, but for tonight he was too drained physically and mentally. He let out a long slow breath and just listened to the sound of it. It felt good as it seemed to take away some of his inner tension. He did it again. He was actually relaxing a little, which finally allowed a restful sleep, something he hadn't had for a very long time.

"Good morning Lisa," said Eddie as he walked into the kitchen rather early the next morning.

"Good morning Eddie. Sleep okay?"

"Yeah, I slept real well. That bed is comfortable."

"Oh yeah, we got a new mattress recently and it's quite nice. Are you hungry? I'm making eggs and bacon. George loves them. I've got plenty if you want some."

"Yeah thanks. Can I help?"

"Can you cook or do you want to pour the coffee?"

"I'd better pour the coffee. We'll all be safer that way," Eddie joked. He was surprised to hear himself talking so comfortably and lightly, but that's how he felt. And it felt good.

"Okay," laughed Lisa. The sugar is in that cupboard," she said, pointing.

Just at that moment George walked in and sat down with his morning paper.

"Don't let the paper fool you, Eddie. George does hold a conversation while he's reading. He's rather talented that way."

Eddie loved to see the nice rapport these two people

shared. It kind of reminded him of Bill and Jan – he liked that. Staring at them without meaning to be obvious he was still trying to understand why they had bailed him out of jail. Why would they do that for him, someone they barely knew? And they didn't know what he would do, like steal from them or run away. Heck, he didn't even know himself. They sure would have made somebody good parents. His mind was all over the place with fantasies and dreams that allowed him not to have to worry about the present.

"Lisa is a very good cook. I always let her do the cooking."

"Well, George likes to do the barbecuing when we have one, which is only occasionally, but that's his specialty." Eddie noticed the warm glances that the two shared. It wasn't phony or pretend, just honest caring between them.

Reminiscing for a moment, Eddie realized that the present was very painful, as was his recent past. Actually, most of his life had been painful except for the time he'd lived with Bill and Jan. It had taken quite a while, but after a few years, he had felt comfortable with them and although he seldom let it show, he thought they really cared about him and he knew he had really found a home. In his six years with them, he finally felt good about himself. That was really home and he had two brothers, Jason and Andrew. Eddie still repeated that to himself because in the three years since the fire, he couldn't convince himself that Bill was gone forever.

"Pass the sugar, will you Eddie?"

Shocked back to the present, Eddie sat up straight and said, "Sure George."

After eating two eggs over easy, three pieces of whole wheat toast and some bacon he said, "I guess I've got my appetite back. Thanks Lisa that was really good."

"You're welcome. It's fun to cook for someone who enjoys it."

"Guess you always like to cook for me, right?" George said.

It was a fun, light and teasing atmosphere throughout breakfast with no one reminding him of how he'd messed up his life. They treated him as a friend and welcomed guest and Eddie felt comfortable. Later, while walking around outside, he remembered that his depression, anger, bad attitude and really dumb decisions had created a lot of trouble for him. During those times he didn't really care about himself or anybody else. He was kicked out of high school and the crappy foster home so he passed drugs for food money. Hell, he was already sleeping on the streets and was hungry and cold most of the time. What did people expect him to do? Probably no one would believe him but he didn't really want to pass drugs, but he was so hungry. He didn't want to be nasty to the teachers at school, but he was so angry. He didn't want to get expelled from school for fighting, but fighting released something inside of him.

All day long as he helped out George and Lisa, his troubles were on his mind. He had decided to cut the lawn for George, a way to earn his keep. Besides, he needed some exercise and just something to do. When he finished the lawn, he sat on the front porch alone, waiting for George to return from his half day of work. It was already past three in the afternoon and George said he would be home by five and then they would go into town to pick up a few things for Eddie. His mind still raced back to a comment that George had said. Eddie had asked him why he had bailed him out. Eddie kept repeating George's answer over and over again in his mind. "Because you're worth it."

Eddie didn't even know how to think about those words. The thought made him feel good and it made him feel bad. It conjured up a feeling of something inside and he didn't even know what it was.

As George pulled into the driveway, Eddie walked up to the car to meet him.

"How's it going Eddie?" George asked.

"Okay, I did your grass, but I couldn't find anything to trim with."

"Yeah I see. Grass looks great. Trimmers are in the basement. I needed to repair something. You can do it tomorrow if you want."

"How long before we go into town?"

"I thought we'd go after dinner, around 7:00."

"Good, then I'll trim it now, if that's okay."

Eddie finished the lawn and did a good job. They went into town and bought Eddie some clothes since he had nothing good to wear, with Eddie vowing that when he got his life straightened out he would pay him back.

"Wanted to talk to you about school. We've got to get you back into school."

"How can you do that? I'm expelled and I'm waiting for my trial." Eddie showed disgust in his tone and obviously couldn't see any possibilities ahead for him. George, on the other hand, talked as if Eddie had many possibilities.

"We've got to get you back in school."

"How? They won't let me."

"Don't know until you try Eddie. If I could find a way, I

want to know what you would do."

Eddie thought for a moment. He still had his dreams but they didn't seem attainable. "What's the use George, really. What's the use?"

"Listen to me Eddie. If you could go back to school, would you want to? Can you put all the bad things aside for a few minutes and if you could, think about it, what would you choose to do?"

"Yeah, I'd go back to school and stay away from all the trouble. Then I'd graduate and probably go on to college. Big hopes, right?"

"Okay, then we start investigating possibilities from the positive point of view. We investigate like they're going to happen, not from the point of view that they're not going to happen – understand? You have to view your life from the position that nothing can stop you from your goals, get it?"

Eddie sat there feeling confused. His thoughts tried to make sense of George's words, but logic avoided him. Finally he said, "Okay then."

"Okay what?" said George. "What do you want to do?"

"I definitely want to finish high school."

"Okay then, that's what I needed to know. I know some people. I could try to get you back in, probably on probation and they would really watch you. Should I try?"

"Really?" said Eddie with the first bit of excitement he felt in a while, " you think you can?"

"Let me try."

"Okay, but what if my trial says jail?"

"Don't know. We'll have to wait and see about that. Let's just see if we can get you back in school for now."

Since they lived in an entirely different school district from the one where Eddie was expelled and since George was a policeman in very good standing, he went and talked to the principal at Lincoln High. Eddie was reinstated on probation but not before he and George had a private meeting with John Beyner, the principal, to set all of the ground rules. And they were very tough but Eddie agreed. He started school the following Monday. He had to start at the beginning of Grade 11, since he had lost all of his credits for an entire semester. That was a tough issue for Eddie to face but in a new environment and with people behind him, he found some hope.

# Chapter Three

Although Eddie seemed to be doing well after an entire month, putting every effort into school and home, George and Lisa were worried he hadn't made any friends and didn't get into any school activities. Eddie responded that he liked it this way, at least until after his trial. He just wanted to study and try to catch up on what he had missed and besides, he was with kids all day long. He seemed more upbeat than down, but was he pretending that things were better than they were? The Bowers didn't know for sure.

One night when George was looking for Eddie, he heard a noise behind the garage. Luckily he recognized the sound before he made his presence known and Eddie was crying his heart out. George stood hidden for a short moment, surprised, yet not surprised. Eddie cried very deeply. It seemed like years of bottled up tears were coming out and along with painful sobs were groans of utter despair. Finally George retreated unnoticed to the house and conferred with Lisa. They knew he kept his emotions inside. George had been hoping that Eddie would start to open up a little, yet maybe letting years of pain out through tears was what he needed. Other times when Eddie was missing for a few hours, they wondered if this scene was repeated.

Had they made a mistake? Eddie appeared to be doing okay, although he had a bit of an attitude at times. Overall his demeanor was that of any teenager in transition stages with his manners sometimes rude but when he remembered, they became kinder. His dress could be sloppy but in style, and his language was quite acceptable.

Eddie had been quiet during the last week, giving revised concern to the Bowers. Neither had been able to draw Eddie out much; he still kept to himself. The bouts of crying had been worrisome with no hint of trouble being discussed. At times he got a little wordy and able to express himself but that was not an usual occurrence. Tonight he was very late for dinner and he hadn't called which was not like him.

"I know you're worried George – what should we do?"

"Just wait, I guess. I'd really like to know what's going on with him, but he's so withdrawn and secretive lately. Never gives himself away. Do you think he's even more quiet than usual now?"

"He's hard to read George."

"Talking doesn't seem to do it with him. We've talked and talked to him so many times, telling him how much we care. How can we show him so he'd believe us?"

"Seems to me that he has to experience or feel something to start believing again."

"How do we help him do that, Lisa?"

"I don't know. I really don't know."

"These last couple of years he's been a tough guy. He had to be and now with all that's happened, well I think he's just so lost." George kept thinking out loud hoping a new idea would materialize to give them a new angle.

"George, we've got to get him into counseling."

150

"If he'll go. It was hard to hear him crying like that but he must have so much inside. God, I hope he didn't run."

"How long should we wait?"

"At least tomorrow – but it's gonna be a long night."

"What would possess him? He has nowhere to go."

"Yeah, but he's really scared and not thinking straight. The trial is getting closer, and heh, what's that?"

Both were very quiet for a moment, listening and hoping that they had heard someone coming.

"Guess it was nothing. Damn, if he runs, we've got more legal problems. I think he could probably get community service and probation on that drug charge, especially if he showed potential and he's been acting real good, but if he runs... well..."

"Let's just wait and see. More coffee, George?"

"No thanks. Things were very rough at that last foster home from what I've heard. I know he just needs a chance but I wonder how long it will take for him to believe in people again and in himself."

"Good question. How do you get to a kid like that?"

"I wish I knew Lisa; I guess just a little at a time. Gees, I hope he didn't run."

"I'm tired, what time is it? Oh, after 10:30, guess we may just as well get ready for bed. Sure hope he's okay."

As for Eddie, when he left school this Thursday, he was feeling very unsure of himself and of his future. He kept thinking, *My trial date is only two weeks away and I've got to make a decision. Should I stay and face the judge with a real possibility of going to jail? Should I run now while I have the chance?*

School was okay and Eddie was doing well. He was thinking, *I like the Bowers but how long will they want me around? I know I can't count on them and I don't totally trust them either. They've been good to me but for how long? And why did they bail me out? There has to be a reason.*

Eddie reminisced, realizing that he had been making his own decisions since he was about six years old. He mostly felt all alone and that's not the way that life was supposed to be. He believed that in those very young years a person was supposed to have a loving mother or a loving father or both. Eddie had neither and as he thought about all the different homes he had lived in he knew it wasn't supposed to be that way. He was just different from other kids and now, at sixteen years old, he had to make another important decision, alone as usual. Life really sucked. He again thought of ending it all but quickly dropped that idea as he realized he could just go somewhere else and start over again. Yeah, he could start over again and again like he was always forced to do.

"Eddie, Eddie." He stopped as he heard a familiar voice calling him. "So this is where you ended up."

Eddie turned to see the familiar face of Tim Harrington. He was the supposed friend of his that ran the other way when they had gotten caught on the drug bust.

"How's it going buddy?" Tim always acted as if he had just found a long time friend.

"Okay, what are you doing here? Are you starting this school?" Eddie shuddered at the thought. He was sorry Tim had found him since he was reminded of a very sad time in his life. Secretly Eddie hoped Tim would just disappear. A lot of his latest dumb decisions and ideas were connected with Tim, a face and time he would just like to forget forever.

"Naw, naw, not going here. My dad put me away in a private school. Got the day off. How did you end up with the judge?"

"Don't know yet. How about you?"

"Don't know, but my dad is going to contribute to some charity or other so I should be okay."

"Oh." Eddie was surprised that he had little to say to Tim anymore.

"I got more stuff last week – are you interested?"

"Are you crazy, Tim?"

"Eddie, it's not really a big deal. Relax a little, will you? We're under age you know. They're not gonna put us in jail or anything. Good fast money."

Eddie couldn't believe his ears. He was at it again, right after being caught. Eddie realized that Tim was just following him as he walked toward the bus stop.

"Does your dad know you're pushing again?"

"Oh no, no. I told you he put me in this private school, you know. What a laugh. More users there cause these kids have more money."

"Hmmm," said Eddie not even bothering to look over at Tim.

Thinking to himself he thought, *I can't believe I was*

*ever like Tim, not really, not inside where it counts. How did I allow myself to get involved with him? I know, it was my decision and I'm responsible, but I don't want to be like him anymore. He's a loser, a liar, and a dealer and he's heading nowhere and I'm not going to be part of this again.*

"So are you with me or no?" Eddie heard such urgency in Tim's tone. He was looking for another victim to do his dirty work. Probably this time, he wouldn't get his own hands dirty but just let someone else do the pushing and if they got caught, he would deny he knew them or had anything to do with it. Well, at least Tim had gotten smarter. But Eddie thought he was smarter too. He was also smart enough not to anger Tim whom he felt could be dangerous.

"Not right now. I want to see what happens at my trial."

"Oh gees, Eddie, you're really sweating that. I can't believe it."

"Well, yeah Tim, I'm really worried, aren't you?"

"Naw, my old man will get me off."

"Well, I don't have an old man to get me off."

"How did you get out anyway, Eddie?"

Eddie didn't want to answer that question. As he paused for a moment, thinking what kind of answer he could give Tim, someone in the distance called Tim's name and off he went without a backward glance. He usually seemed to be dashing here and there, always aware of everyone around. He was not very tall but very strong with a loud voice that someone once said he developed to make up for his small stature.

Eddie drew a sigh of relief and actually allowed himself to listen as he let out his breath very slowly. He had played along a little so as not to get on Tim's bad side and he had succeeded in that. What worried Eddie was that Tim would always be around and what would happen the next time if he said no again? Tim had lots of contacts and friends and he could make it real tough on you. No one wanted to be on Tim's bad list.

On the ride home, Eddie stared out the window of the bus to a world that seemed like it was as much in a daze as he was. He didn't know what was real and what was make believe. *What is real for me,* he wondered? *What in my whole life has been real? I don't know anymore. But I know that I have to get away. I don't want to be associated with the Tims of the world and I don't want to go to jail.*

Eddie got off at the next bus stop, miles from his destination. He didn't know what he wanted to do but he didn't want to go home right now. He had to think. Home still didn't have much meaning for him but fear did and Eddie was scared. When he thought too much, he got scared and then he couldn't think clearly. Now he was almost in a panic and he just had to get away. He didn't even have a plan. Where would he go? Decisions were so tough for him lately. But he knew he wasn't going home.

Hours later found Eddie still walking around and very tired. Walking always helped him think, but today, he was so agitated that nothing seemed to work. Finally he found a park and sat down on one of the benches. He took a deep breath and again listened to himself exhale. Then he just sat. Thoughts were not coming easily and his mind seemed to be on strike against any useful thinking. So he just sat on the old brown colored bench enjoying the trees and slightly aware of the scent of nearby flowers. A light breeze enveloped his tired body and gently coaxed his mind back to the present moment. A rather old gentleman walking by decided to sit down at the other end of the bench. He was dressed casually but nicely and had a pleasant face. Eddie guessed him around seventy-five. The two just sat there in silence, tending to their own thoughts as they watched the strollers in the park slowly pass them by.

Eddie realized it was almost seven o'clock. George and Lisa would be worried about him. He had an urge to call but felt he couldn't until he had cleared his thoughts and made a decision. If he decided to run, he would call them to let them know – he did owe them that much, and the more he thought about it he realized that running was his only choice. He could start heading toward Indiana where Jan and Jason and Andrew had moved. He knew he would be welcome there. He always felt more comfortable and cheerful around them although the dark cloud inside him now probably wouldn't totally disappear, ever. Still it was a plan and he liked it. He could get a job, hang low until he reached eighteen, and maybe even finish high school and live a good life.

Thump, thump. Eddie looked over startled out of his thoughts to see what caused the noise to the left of him. He heard the man at the end of the bench groan and then saw him fall over on his shoulder. Then he didn't move.

"Sir, sir. Are you okay?"

No answer. No movement.

"Sir, sir, is anything wrong?" Eddie said and this time he spoke very loud.

No answer. No movement.

Eddie got up hurriedly and went over to the man and shook him gently to see if he could get any reaction. No reaction.

"Sir, sir?" Eddie bent down hoping to see some movement on his face, eyes blinking or an expression of some kind. There was none.

Eddie felt for a pulse. Bill Conrad had insisted his boys learn CPR and life saving skills. He just wanted them to be prepared. Eddie was sure Bill was watching him now from somewhere. Finally someone was approaching.

"Do you have a phone?" he yelled. "Call 911, this man just fell over and he barely has a pulse."

As Eddie heard the call for a 911 operator, he loosened the man's collar. Then he got instructions and cleared the air passages and started CPR. In less than five minutes, the paramedics arrived and took over. The old man didn't have an ID on him so thinking that Eddie was with him, they insisted he go to the hospital. Eddie tried to tell them that he didn't know the man, but to no avail. Eddie found himself going to the hospital.

Now he was thinking again and realizing that he probably wasn't going to run away today. Maybe something just didn't want him to go, he thought. Life was short but really precious, and you never knew what was ahead for you. Actually no one did. Look at this man, out for a stroll, stopped to sit on a bench and look what happened.

Eddie was looking at his life differently. Maybe it was the shock of the last few hours' activities. If he ran away, he could possibly run into a much worse situation. At this moment, he couldn't really imagine his life worse but he did have George and Lisa in his corner, at least for now, and they were good to him. He had a good place to live, good meals and maybe he'd luck out in court. After all, he knew what to expect here but he didn't know what he'd find on the road.

Finally convincing the attendants and staff at the hospital that he didn't know the man, they all marveled that this man was lucky someone who knew CPR was around. They related that he had suffered a heart attack and added that Eddie's knowledge of CPR had probably saved his life. The man, Charles Ingle, was in the emergency room, awake but shaky, and he wanted to see Eddie.

"Only for a few seconds," said the nurse, "and then maybe you won't be so agitated."

"Young man I don't know how to thank you."

"It's okay," said Eddie, "I'm glad I could help."

"They tell me if it wasn't for you knowing CPR I might not be here now."

Just then the head nurse came in, angry that Charles seemed to be holding a conversation at this time and so she rushed Eddie out of the room. Eddie did promise that he would come back in the next couple of days. With that, Eddie left.

What should he do now? He had planned to run away, but now, honestly he didn't feel like it. He actually felt good and his spirits were raised up. He had actually helped to save somebody's life. That was a pretty amazing feeling. He thought of George and Lisa and had a fleeting thought that maybe that's how they felt about him. He wasn't exactly saved yet, but Eddie could see the Bowers were trying. Wow – his entire body trembled in a new realization that was entering his mind. *I have to call the Bowers. They might be mad, as they have a right to be, but I don't want them to worry anymore and something real good has happened to me and I want to share it with them.*

When the phone rang, George and Lisa just looked at each other. George expected bad news when he picked up the receiver and so he answered softly. But instead, he heard the voice of Eddie with a fresh almost excited tone. Eddie related what happened and how he had handled it and ended up at the hospital. He hoped they weren't too worried and said that he had a lot to discuss with them tonight or tomorrow. The paramedics had offered to drive him home and they would be leaving shortly.

After George related the entire incident as he knew it to Lisa, they both knew why he had been in that park walking around. They knew he probably contemplated running away, but he was coming back for now. That's all that mattered.

"His voice sounded so different Lisa, like it had new life in it. He almost sounded happy and definitely excited. It was good to hear him sound like that."

"He must be proud of helping to save someone's life."

"Yeah," said George, "that must be it."

A little while later as he walked up the steps to his home, Eddie thought about the conversation he'd had with the paramedics.

"You did a good job, Eddie. Lucky for Mr. Ingle that you knew what to do. How do you feel?"

"It's a great feeling, isn't it? "

"Now you know how we feel, almost every day."

"Yeah, wow." That last line stayed with Eddie.

After he had related step by step the entire story of his rescue with tons of pride in his voice, he fell silent and casually turned to another topic.

"I want to be honest with both of you. I had thoughts of running away. In fact I started to and was thinking of taking a bus to Indiana, but then I didn't cause I wasn't sure."

"To see Jan and the boys?"

"Yeah, when I think of them I feel good and remember happier times."

"Why did you turn back?"

"After I helped that man I really felt different inside and for a little while, that dark shadow I usually have was gone. There were a couple of other reasons too. Both of you went out on a limb for me and George said something else to me. You know what he said Lisa?"

"What?"

"Well, I asked him why he did it, why he bailed me out like that and he looked me right in the eyes and said, 'cause you're worth it.'

"I agree with George," said Lisa smiling at him.

"But you people don't even know me – not really."

"I'm not surprised you saved that man. You could have just run then, but you didn't. You could have just left him, Eddie, but you're not like that. We knew Bill and Jan; Bill and I used to talk about you. I've sort of kept up with your life through Bill and at basketball. Did you know that I was in the police station that night you were brought in at four years old?"

"No," said Eddie looking up at George, feeling a quick shock run through his body. "You were there?"

"Yes I was and you were a very brave little boy. But you were so alone. We all hoped your mom would come and get you and no one knows for sure why she couldn't come back."

"Yeah, she never came back. She never even called."

"Maybe she couldn't. There might have been a reason. But that's in the past. Why were you thinking of running away?"

"I'm just really scared, you know. I know I'm not supposed to say that because I'm a guy, but I get real scared sometimes. What if I don't make it again? What if I have to go to jail. I'm not sure I could handle that."

"I get scared Eddie, a lot of times. We all do. We don't know what's going to happen, but when you get scared, why don't you talk to us? That's why we're here. We care about you."

"I'm beginning to believe you. I don't know why. It's only been a couple of months so why should you care what happens to me? Don't get me wrong cause I'm glad to have a nice place to stay and food every day, but I don't want to get too used to it."

"Actually, I feel I've known you for a long time. If Bill hadn't died, you know that you'd still be with him and his family, right? Why not take a chance on us? Besides, where would you go if you ran?"

"Well, like I said, my final destination would be Indiana but maybe just another state right now. I thought they probably wouldn't come after me for passing drugs. But of course, they might."

"And then you'd always be looking over your shoulder."

"Yeah, that's true too. But I didn't go, did I? I felt I'd be alone again. And even though things aren't very permanent in my life, I kind of like it here, at least while it lasts."

George said. "We like having you here but we're a team and watch out for each other. That goes for you too."

"How can we help?" asked Lisa. "How can we make it better for you?"

"I don't know, maybe just more time. But on the ride back here I decided I'm not running again. That'd be stupid. I have to say here and face a few things and maybe get my record straight again. I might have a chance then. So if it's okay, I'm staying with you."

"You'll always have a home with us," said George.

Eddie looked as deeply as he could into George and Lisa's facial expressions. He wanted to find something that would convince him that they really wanted him to stay. They said the right words but he couldn't quite get the confirming feeling inside of him.

"I'd like to go to my room now, finish my homework and get some sleep. I've got school tomorrow."

As he started walking out of the room, Eddie had a feeling for one more statement that was on his mind. "I know I still have problems and I know I've lots to make up for. I personally think life can be pretty crappy, but right now, I do have a good place to stay with nice people and I'm happy about that. Thanks."

"We like having you here. Good night."

Less than two days later, Tim Harrington was arrested on drug possession and this time there was no bail and his father couldn't donate his way out. It was juvenile court immediately and off to a maximum juvenile home, no bail, to await trial.

The next day Eddie wanted to talk again. Eddie hadn't showed outward anger but George could tell he had been using a lot of control and not always winning.

"Looks like Tim is out of your life, at least for now. But there are always other Tims out there."

"Not for me. I've been thinking about my life like you said. But I want to tell you something else first. After Bill died and I went to that foster home, I almost died inside – it was such a terrible place. They have drug addicts all over the place, no supervision, no rule; it's just a real bad place, George. I'm not making excuses for my bad decisions, that's my fault alone, but that place made it very hard to stay straight."

"I know some people right now trying to close it down."

"Yeah, that's good to hear," said Eddie, staring in the distance as if in private memories. "Some people there are really bad, but some are good kids and they don't have a chance. I think I was pretty good when I first went there but now, well..."

Eddie looked down and went off on his own for a few long moments. He felt a sudden jar back to the present. "I did try, you know, in spite of it all, I tried hard but kids at school, well, you couldn't hang around with good kids if you lived in that place. They didn't want to have anything to do with you. And you couldn't play sports hanging around with the others. It's a lose/lose situation. I say, get those other kids out of that home. Give them a chance."

"Maybe we could work together getting that to happen."

For the first time he saw a look of satisfaction on George's face. Once when he was talking about the life saving incident, he saw the same look but then it was gone. Now it was back again.

"I'd like to finish school but it may take more time for me to catch up. When you asked me what would I like to do if I could do anything?"

163

"Yeah, what?"

"Well, even when I was with Bill, I didn't expect to play basketball forever. I know I was pretty good but would probably never made it as a pro. And I didn't want that anyway. I wanted to make a difference with other kids like me. Nobody really understands how it feels to be abandoned and given away, except others like me. I thought I could make a difference."

"That's great Eddie. How do you feel now about doing something like that?"

"I don't feel that I can even think about it right now. Here in your house I'm okay. Things are good. But when I look back at my life and my world, I'm furious. I didn't cooperate with those teachers at school because I was always so angry inside. You can't know how I feel and I've got to find a way to deal with it."

"How do you plan to do that?"

"I don't know. I just don't know. I've known for a while that my anger gets me into trouble, but sometimes I just get so angry all of a sudden, with no real idea where it came from. It's like life makes me mad."

"Sounds like a good place to start inside yourself."

"But I've thought about it a lot and don't know what to do. How does a person change?"

"Slowly, with the proper help. You probably should have talked to someone a long time ago about it but you didn't get the chance."

That statement put Eddie in a very thoughtful mood. He was thinking about options and possibilities but couldn't see any.

"How, George?"

"Counseling. We need you to talk to someone who can help you deal with these feelings and find a better and more appropriate reaction for you."

"Like a shrink? Maybe I'm crazy."

"No, no, no. That's what a lot of people think but no. If a person had cancer, they wouldn't go see a teacher. If a person had a foot disease, they wouldn't go to a hand doctor. You need someone to help you with your emotions."

Eddie just sat and looked at George. But he did listen.

"When your mom left you in that park, that started a cycle of confusion, anger and inner pain. It would for anyone. You've never had a chance to deal with it. I think you should and that it would make a difference."

"Really, you think someone could help me with that?"

"Yes, I do. Let me as you a question. When you were with Bill and Jan, I know you were doing great and accomplished a lot. Maybe if Bill had lived you would have been okay. But tell me, how did you feel inside during those years? Can you remember?"

Eddie sat back on the couch and resumed his thoughtful position. Eddie liked to have his head resting on one hand on his cheek and stretch out his legs. "You know, that's good. I was happy there later on. But at first I was very slow to get close to anyone. That was always hard for me. I know I always pushed people away, probably still do, but I can't help that. It's just the way I am. I mean, nothing ever lasts in my life. That didn't last either, although it wasn't anyone's fault."

"Sometimes things happen."

"Yeah, but even later when I got more comfortable with them and felt that this just might last, even then, there was always this, ummm, like a cloud, yeah, like a dark cloud never letting me enjoy them to the fullest. I never really thought about this for a while, but at my eleventh birthday party I remember it because it was such a beautiful day. I made my wish and wouldn't tell anyone because I knew they wouldn't understand. Anyway, I would have been embarrassed. I wished that I could totally enjoy the day or the moment for once without having this dark shadow inside of me. Sounds crazy, huh?"

"Not crazy at all. Must be hard living with that."

"But it lessened a lot during those years with the Conrads. But it came back stronger than ever after Bill died."

"Yeah, I can understand that."

Eddie really believed that George could understand.

"Eddie would you go talk to someone? They're people who deal with kids just like you and would know how to help you."

"Nobody would have to find out, right? I know I've done stupid things but I don't want people to think I'm totally crazy."

"Nobody would have to know."

"That's good. Maybe I should, huh? You think I should, George?"

"I think it would be worth a try to understand and get rid of the dark shadows you talk about."

"Yep, that might be worth a try. That's a hard feeling to understand but it's always there trying to depress me."

"Let me talk to a friend of mine and find what's best for you."

"Okay, well okay. You know something else?"

"What Eddie?"

"I'd like to write to Jan sometime. Not right away, but later. I'd like to write to her."

"That's good. I know she'd love to hear from you."

"She wouldn't like what I've done and what I've become."

"She loves you Eddie we all do."

"Then why do I think I'm a loser? I feel like such a loser."

"No Eddie, you're not a loser. You've gone the wrong way with no one to help you in hard times, but you're not a loser."

Eddie just sat there, lost in his own thoughts. He liked the words he was hearing; he just wished he could believe them.

"You know what else Eddie?"

"What?" he said in a very soft, thoughtful tone of voice.

"You're not alone anymore either."

Eddie felt his face shift as he felt like smiling. Eddie and George just looked at each other for a moment. They weren't smiling really, but there was an appreciation of each other in their expression. It was one of those moments in time.

Eddie asked George to go to the hospital with him to visit Charles Ingle. As they arrived, his wife was just leaving.

"Oh you're Eddie Sabers. I can't thank you enough for helping my husband. My entire family is so grateful. May I give you a hug?" Eddie stood there rather embarrassed but accepted the hug with compassion for the lady. "I hope to see you again soon. I know Charles wants to stay in touch with you."

"Your very welcome Mrs. Ingle. I'm very pleased that I was able to help."

Then Eddie introduced Charles to George and he had to sit there for the first ten minutes of the visit listening to these two men singing his praises. Eddie fought hard to keep the tears back but noticed that Charles had tears in his eyes too. Before they left Mr. Ingle's vowed to keep in touch with Eddie and hoped to take him out to dinner sometime.

"It's a very small and inadequate payment for saving someone's life, but I would like to remain connected to my new friend, okay?"

"I'd like that too Mr. Ingle. I really would but I do have a few problems to sort out first."

Eddie told Charles about his problems. Mr. Ingle was so easy to talk to. He wanted to know if he could help in any way but Eddie said he was facing his past mistakes since that was the only way that he knew how to go forward with his life.

On his court date morning, Eddie woke up very tired. He hadn't slept much, not at all really, and he was quite nervous. He tried to eat breakfast but for once he wasn't hungry and just waited while George finished. Eddie had to miss school but had taken extra homework to make it up. If only he got his chance, he would make good on it.

Being called before the judge with George at his side was much easier than the first time when he had been here alone. He wasn't alone this time. Eddie had people who cared for him and he was a different kid now. This difference was not lost on the judge who gave Eddie three years' probation and one hundred hours of community service. That was a surprise and a big relief. The other surprise was that Mr. Ingle found out about Eddie's court date and sent his testimony to the judge. That had helped the judge's decision too. Even the judge was happy. He knew that Eddie was back on the good side of the fence again and didn't want to get in his way. But he cautioned him to use what would probably be his last chance constructively and intelligently and with that brought down his gavel.

The biggest plus for Eddie was that he had a good place to live with people who cared about him and a good focus on life. He walked out of that courtroom with tears in his eyes, but new enthusiasm in his footsteps and a vow to himself to straighten out his life for good.

Eddie attended counseling groups for abandoned and neglected children and also had one-on-one therapy. He was surprised to realize that he was not the only one who had dark shadows inside. He was not the only one to have so much anger and trouble controlling it. As it turned out, many other abandoned kids had very similar problems and these other kids knew exactly how Eddie felt inside because they'd been there too. Even their group leader was adopted and Eddie developed a strong connection with him. He learned that this inner pain and these dark shadows never go away entirely. Who could forget that their mom gave them away or walked away without a backward glance? Yet everyone seemed to learn in time how to live with the past while creating a good and meaningful future for themselves. Everyone's story had different details, but the basic facts were the same. It was great to talk to others who understood. It helped a lot.

Eddie did a lot of serious thinking during this time in his life. *My mom is still on my mind now and then, but I'm not obsessed about her anymore. I can accept the fact that the old questions still cross my mind. What possessed her to just leave me in the park that day? And who was she with? It couldn't have been my father. Or was it? Did they both want to leave me behind? I'm happy I can think of my birth parents and still maintain control of my emotions. The only thing that irritates me is that I'll never be able to ask them what happened. Certainly not my father, but not even my mother. No one knows who she is. I have no point to even start to look for her. I don't want to have an angry confrontation with her anymore or to tell her what I truly think of what she did. I moved beyond that point a long time ago. But I wish that I would get a chance to understand why. That's all I want to know. What was happening in her life at that time that she felt it was better to just leave me in a park and not come back. I'd like to know that. Maybe it would help. Maybe not.*

Looking back on his life, Eddie felt he was a lucky guy. He chose to accept and believe that his mom just didn't have a choice. Inside his being, he could live with that thought and that's what he chose to think. And look what happened to him. He had so many people that cared about him, so many good people who stood behind him and cheered him on, all through his life. He was one lucky guy. Now he sat and smiled smugly to himself. He had a new line that he wanted to shout to the world and it was, EDDIE SABERS HAS MANY PEOPLE WHO CARE ABOUT HIM. His life had changed for the better; he had been given a wonderful chance to make a difference. He thanked them with all his heart and knew from now on, Eddie Sabers was going in the right direction.

In a very short time Eddie mentioned to George. "Now that my community service is finished I've been looking back on the places I've worked. I did thirty hours at that home for the aged and I think I helped make some of them smile every day. I did another thirty hours each at an orphanage and a foster home. But when they gave me a choice as to where to finished my last ten hours, I was glad to go to that under-financed foster home."

"What did you think of that place?"

"It's a good home just not a rich one, but I think they do a good job there making the kids believe they really care about them. I think I made a difference too."

"You did good, Eddie, congratulations. Are you ready for your graduation from high school?

"Oh yeah, and I'm glad everyone's coming. Jan has really improved so she can make the trip here to see me graduate with Andrew and Jason. That's so special. I had such fun visiting them last year. And I just got a letter from Andrew and he'll be starting his third year of college in the fall. Time is moving on for all of us."

"I'm very proud of you Eddie. You've done well."

"Thanks, George. I've so many people to thank for that and you and Lisa are among them too. Did I tell you that I've been asked to give the commencement address? Can you believe it?"

"No kidding. That's great."

"Yeah, I just found out and I'm really surprised. You know it's usually one of the top kids in school. I mean the one with the highest GPA or the class president or a big sports hero. But I'm not anything like that. But the kids vote and they voted for me to speak."

"Gees. How fantastic, Eddie. How do you feel, nervous, excited? Do you have any idea what you're going to say?"

"I've got some thoughts but nothing tangible yet. But I've got a couple of weeks yet to figure it out. I want to give a real good speech."

"I'm sure you will, Eddie. I'm sure you will."

Eddie was nervous on the morning of the graduation. He was graduating a year later than most of his fellow graduates, but that was okay. He was so thrilled to graduate at all. He had become a very popular kid with the teachers, other students and even with the counselors. To others he was recognized as a natural leader. Eddie didn't see that within himself but others did. The day moved on slowly but they all arrived at the auditorium of the school and as Eddie looked out from behind the stage he saw Jan, Jason and Andrew Conrad, as well as Lisa and George Bowers. The surprise was Charles and his wife Betty Ingle and his family were also all sitting together out in the audience. He felt tears well up inside of him when suddenly he heard his name called and stepped out on the platform and headed for the podium quickly before he had time to think and get nervous about the situation. He did stop for a moment, just long enough to look upward briefly, then proceeded amidst thunderous applause.

"Thank you. I'd like to address the faculty members, parents, relatives, friends and my fellow students. We made it, didn't we?" The applause again was deafening. "Yes, we made it to our high school graduation and we are all very proud as we should be. We all worked hard, some harder than others, to get here today each one of us in our own way. Most of you know my story but I'd like to share with you again in hopes that I can make a difference, because if I can, then we all can. My mom dropped me off at a playground and never came back. I was four years old. I just wanted to tell her today, wherever she is, I forgive you mom. I may never understand why you did what you did, but I forgive you. I'm nineteen years old now. I spent the first years of my life angry and furious at my mom. From there it went into rage and fury as I went from one foster home to another. I hated life and it wasn't fair to me as far as I could tell. But later I learned that life just is. You make it what you want for yourself. Around seven years old, I did luck out. I got moved to the foster home of Bill and Jan Conrad. I acknowledge and applaud you Jan, who is here with us today."

Eddie started a round of applause that didn't end until Jan stood up in acknowledgement. "In this home I learned about trust, love and acceptance; all of the things I never before experienced. I also gained two brothers and found out what it meant to care about each other. I was not an easy kid to live with in the beginning, but they never gave up on me. Thanks Jan and you too Bill, wherever you are. Then we had a house fire and Bill died. I was almost fourteen. Jan was hurt and couldn't go on and since I wasn't officially adopted yet, I couldn't stay with her. I want to tell you all that it was a very dark moment of my life. I got moved to a very bad foster home, no supervision and lived among drug addicts and drug pushers and I again became very angry toward life and did some very stupid things. Then at probably the lowest point in my life I again made the acquaintance of George and Lisa Bowers." They had to stand up amidst more applause. "They bailed me out of jail, believed in me when no one else did. Even I didn't believe in me but they took a chance on me. I want to tell you faculty, parents, teachers and my fellow students that you see me before you today, a graduate who was voted to give this graduation address because of the people I just mentioned. We all need someone who cares about us. In our darkest moments, we especially need someone who will believe in us, when we don't even believe in ourselves."

At that last sentence Eddie had to stop briefly, his voice was cracking and it took a moment for him to recover. It also gave the audience a chance to start applauding again, at first slowly, then it picked up more speed until finally everyone was on their feet and just continued applauding as no one wanted this moment to end. Everyone was together in feelings and understanding. It was a magical time.

"Thank you. Thank you. I really don't know where I'd be today without George and Lisa Bowers who picked me up from the dark basement of my world and brought me up to see there was light. So many of you say I touched your lives and to you I say, thank you, thank you for the chance. I sat and laughed with some of you; I cried with others and just sat and held others who needed not to feel alone. Why? Why did I get good at this as you all say I did? It was because I had great role models in my life. I want you to know how important another human being can be in one's life. Charles Ingle sits out there as a very dear friend and he says that I saved his life. I know you all know about that incident. Yet Charles doesn't know he saved my life that same day because I was planning to run away. Yes, I was going to run away because I was scared, and what would I run to? I didn't know. There was nothing better out there. I had potential here with people who cared about me. So I want to thank Charles Ingle for saving my life as I was saving his life.

"So my fellow student and friends, know that you all have potential. Know that you can be

174

whatever you want to be. Dream big dreams and expect them all to come true. Yet remember along the way the importance of every human being. Know how much difference each one of us can make. I have had two main sets of people in my life who got me all the way to graduation. I still thank my mom for giving birth to me, but my other sets of parents gave me the daily love and nurturing that allowed me to grow and survive.

"Never, never underestimate the power you have, each one of you to help another human being feel important, worthwhile and special. Please, please remember how much difference one person can make in another's life. Go out and make that difference wherever and whenever you get the chance. Then, don't even worry about being happy and being successful after you graduate; you'll already be there.

"Thank you everyone, and I want to thank all the parents, teachers and relatives out there who got us all to graduation. Thank you EVERY ONE."

The applause was one of the longest ever given in a graduation address at that school. People just couldn't settle down and just kept applauding and standing. No one even sat back down. Eddie touched a soft note in the graduates but also in every faculty member, parent, relative and friend. Eddie had made his difference that would not soon be forgotten. Bill would have been so proud of his role model.

George and Lisa went to talk to Jan. Most couldn't even find words to say. They just stood there looking at each other. Finally George spoke in a very cautious voice.

"Who could have possibly known?" That was all he said and it was enough.

It would be great to tell you that Eddie went to college and graduated at the top of his class cum laude with all the highest honors, but he didn't. Yet Eddie is presently in his third year at college, carrying a B average and always working part time. He is not a straight A student, but he does well and is very dedicated. He is studying mechanical engineering with a minor in psychology. He has become a part-time paramedic and has helped save a few more lives. Eddie still lives with George and Lisa, at least until he finishes college, but he spends his summers and many holidays in Indiana. For a kid just dropped off and abandoned, he has a good family and many friends spread out in two different states.

Eddie Sabers has made a difference in his world and Eddie is still a positive difference that can be felt.

# EPILOGUE

Regardless of the past insults in their lives or possibly because of them, these children are making a positive difference in their world. That is not to say they lived happily ever after, so few do. But they were given their chance and what they did could surprise you.

Lindsey made it through a prestigious college, easily graduating with a degree in Accounting. She went on to get a Master's Degree and is presently working in an accounting firm where she's had two promotions in the past two years and her financial future seems secure. She's a hard worker and is also applauded for her consideration of other people. Sometimes Lindsey wonders what would have happened to her if she had not been put in Ms. April Munson's special class. She says she can't imagine. Without the skillful help of a therapist who understood her, Lindsey believes she wouldn't have had control of her emotions and her relationships, both working and social. Acknowledging that she does have good parents whom she appreciates, Lindsey knows the void in her life, filled mostly by her teacher/therapist April, would have caused her considerable damage. When she remembers the trapped pain she endured as a child, she realizes that presently it is only a passing thought and still expresses surprise that she can view everything rather objectively without strong emotions. The proof for Lindsey is inside herself and she plans to pass it on whenever she can.

Still single at twenty-eight, Lindsey has a significant other lately that looks promising. She met Richard Pender at a seminar at work and made an instant connection. He is a very sensitive and thoughtful person and they share an interest in their work as well as being supporting of each other's lives. However, she's in no hurry for a commitment since she has a strong purpose and ideal for her life. And most important, she wants to make certain that when she marries and has her own children, she will be ready for them. Her friend, Richard, told Lindsey about his brother-in-law, Eddie Sabers. After meeting they found a commonality that led to special bond which brings them to meetings and seminars and foster homes to help children. Wanting to give back what she feels she was blessed to receive, she works with April and helps when seminars and classes are in session. To be helping parents who are trying to find answers for their struggling children fulfills her desire to give back what she received herself. Of course, Lindsey is a valuable asset with the little children with whom she always has a good rapport. The parents appreciate her input and her uncanny ability to build a bond with even the most troubled youngsters. Lindsey was heading over tonight for another parenting seminar that April was giving in an attempt to educate parents in techniques to use with their troubled kids.

Eddie Sabers played basketball all through his college years satisfying his need to finish what he had started years earlier. He learned how to make good friends with people who had promising goals and definite values in their lives. To this end, Eddie joined the welcoming committee at his college and pushed himself to overcome his desire to stay in the background. And so, he met Linda Pender who was a naturally outgoing participator and helped him to be comfortable on the committee. They made an immediate connection and married soon after graduation. And through his brother-in-law he met Lindsey Hall. Together they progressed in their supportive goal to help other children get the help they needed.

Although Eddie works as an engineer, he continued working as a part-time paramedic. His paramedic days were reduced to volunteer status only recently when he and his wife had their second child. Eddie and his family travel to Indiana at least once a year to spend time with his other relatives and communication thrives between them the rest of the year. His two brothers Andrew and Jason are also married with children and all the cousins have a great time together. Jan's health has improved considerably and she enjoys all of her grandchildren.

George and Lisa Bowers live only a few miles from Eddie. Grandpa is active in his grandchildren's lives and gives them the same great comradeship and values that Eddie received. Some days when Eddie watches George playing with his kids, tears come to his eyes as he remembers back in time. George and Lisa still take in struggling kids and although they never had any children of their own, they are grandparents to quite a few.

Occasionally when he looks back over his life, Eddie believes he was fortunate and is thankful to be where he is today. His birth mother still crosses his mind at times so after a moment or two of quiet reflection, he just wishes her well in a passing thought and moves on. Eddie has never forgotten how the intervention of a few good people made such an important difference in his life and he works hard to give back to his community.

Lindsey arrived at the seminar a few minutes late, a habit she has never broken and rushed over to April letting her know she was here and asking how she could help.

"Hi Ms. April, looks like we're getting a crowd tonight?"

"Yes, word got out on this seminar so I'm glad you're here. Can you look over the roster and make sure there are nametags for the new people on the list?"

"Okay, I'll do that now. I'm excited about being here. You know, I always learn something new at these meetings."

"Me too, none of us know it all," April offered.

Lindsey smiled and said, "Gee, and all these years I thought you did."

April just smiled back at her and continued with her work. Lindsey sat down a few chairs away at the reception table and looked over the roster. Soon she heard another voice over her shoulder.

"Hi Lindsey, I even talked Linda into coming with me tonight."

And there was Eddie Sabers with his wife. Sitting down they were both ready to help and to do whatever they could. As Eddie and Lindsey exchanged a quick knowing glance, they realized something few others could share in their excitement to help another child. They knew how important one person had been in their lives. And this was true for everyone. Everyone needs a friend.